Hearn's Valley

Hearn's Valley

Wayne D. Overholser

THORNDIKE

CHIVERS

This Large Print edition is published by Thorndike Press®, Waterville, Maine USA and by BBC Audiobooks Ltd, Bath, England.

Published in 2005 in the U.S. by arrangement with Golden West Literary Agency.

Published in 2006 in the U.K. by arrangement with Golden West Literary Agency.

U.S. Hardcover 0-7862-7959-1 (Western)
U.K. Hardcover 1-4056-3575-4 (Chivers Large Print)
U.K. Softcover   1-4056-3576-2 (Camden Large Print)

The text of this Large Print edition is unabridged. Other aspects of the book may vary from the original edition.

Set in 16 pt. Plantin by Al Chase.

Printed in the United States on permanent paper.

British Library Cataloguing-in-Publication Data available

Library of Congress Cataloging-in-Publication Data

Overholser, Wayne D., 1906–
    Hearn's Valley / by Wayne D. Overholser.
        p. cm. — (Thorndike Press large print westerns)
    ISBN 0-7862-7959-1 (lg. print : hc : alk. paper)
    1. Large type books. I. Title. II. Thorndike Press large print Western series.
PS3529.V33H43 2005
813'.54—dc22   2005015301

Hearn's Valley

Chapter 1

Hugh Moberly had hated Vic Hearn as long as he could remember, but he had never hated him more than he did on the May evening when he rode into his father's place on the Deschutes and found Hearn standing beside the covered wagon in front of the log house.

Hugh had not been home for more than a year; he had been looking forward to this visit with growing anticipation from the time he'd left The Dalles on the Columbia. Now, to see Hearn standing there with the familiar smile on his lips and his great legs spread, his thumbs hooked under his belt, was more than Hugh could stand.

Hearn raised a hand in greeting when Hugh reined up. "How are you, boy?" he asked in his booming voice. "Where have you been? We sure weren't expecting you."

Not answering, Hugh reined up and remained motionless on his roan gelding for a moment, looking down at Hearn, all the good feeling that had been stored up in him disappearing as quickly as if it were a pile of dust whipped into oblivion by a sudden gust of wind. Anyone looking at Hearn sensed strength and wealth and power; but Hugh saw cruelty there, too, and ruthlessness and brutality.

"Get down, son," Hearn said. "You're home."

Hugh stepped wearily out of the saddle. He took Hearn's proffered hand as he asked, "What are you doing here?"

"Why, who has a better right to be here than me?" Hearn asked, as if surprised by the question. "After all, your mother is almost a sister to me."

It was a lie, Hugh knew, just as nearly everything Hearn did and said when he was here was a lie. The smile, a little strained now, remained on Hearn's lips under the yellow mustache, but the blue eyes were questioning, as if he didn't understand Hugh's attitude and was hurt by it.

Hearn was a big man, as tall as Hugh, and broader of shoulder and deeper of chest, but it wasn't so much the size of the man that set him apart from everyone else as it was his manner of cold competence. Hugh wondered if he had ever failed at anything, or with anyone, except, of course, Hugh's mother.

8

"I know," Hugh said. "I know exactly how you feel about Ma. Where is she?"

"Inside," Hearn said. "Finishing packing."

Hugh turned toward the house, not knowing what Hearn meant when he said she was finishing packing, and not wanting to ask. He stepped through the front door and stopped, his breath coming hard for a moment. His mother's big metal trunk was in the middle of the room, with three leather suitcases and an old carpetbag on the floor beside it. The few good pieces of furniture that his folks owned were gone. So were the books that belonged on the shelves beside the fireplace. His parents' wedding picture that had always hung over the mantel was missing, too.

"Ma." He tried to shout the word, but his throat closed up so that the sound was no more than a hoarse whisper. "Ma." He tried again, but it was no better.

Apparently she heard, for she ran out of the bedroom. She stared at him, shocked motionless by surprise, and Hugh, looking at her, marveled at how neither age nor poverty had touched her. As a boy he had considered her the most beautiful woman in the world, and now, a man, he had not changed his opinion.

"Hugh, oh, Hugh!" she cried. "I didn't hear you ride up."

She crossed the room to him, her arms extended, her face bright with the pleasure of this moment. He forgot Vic Hearn; he could think of nothing except that it was good to be here, good to see her again, good to put strife and bloodshed and bitterness behind him.

He hugged her hard, and kissed her, and she cried a little from sheer happiness, then wiped her eyes and looked up at him. "Seems like you've grown." She ran a hand over his brown hair, and rubbed his week-old stubble with her fingertips. "You need a shave, Hugh." She smiled, her dark eyes meeting his gray ones, then suddenly her face turned grave. "We haven't heard from you for three months. Why didn't you write that you were coming home?"

"I'm sorry, Ma. I aimed to. Just seemed like I never got time. I guess that's a pretty poor excuse, isn't it?"

"Just about the poorest there is," she agreed.

"Where's Pa?"

"In Prineville."

Hugh pointed at the trunk and suitcases. "What's going on?"

She stiffened, and drew away from him as

10

if knowing he would not approve, then motioned toward the worn horsehair sofa. "Sit down, Hugh. I want to talk to you. I've been worried sick about leaving because I didn't know where you were and couldn't let you know. I was going to leave a note on the front door, but if you didn't come for a long time it would get torn off."

He sat down, thinking how many times he had bounced on the sofa when he was a boy. He remembered when his father had hauled it from Prineville, a beautiful piece of furniture. It had been comfortable enough then, and his mother had asked him to help take care of it, but of course he hadn't. He'd jumped on it; he'd used the arms for horses, yelling at the top of his voice while he chased Indians or stampeded cattle, and all the time he was using his father's quirt on it. He'd wrestled with his dog and got hair all over it, and he remembered how angry his mother had been. Well, it wasn't worth much now. He had done more to wear it out in the few years he'd been home than his folks had in all the time they'd had it.

His mother sat down beside him and took one of his hands in both of hers. She didn't say anything for a while, frowning as if trying to sort out the words that were in her mind so that she would pick only the right ones.

Glancing down at her, at the evening sun falling through a west window and touching her black hair, he wondered again how she had been able to defy age the way she had. Though she was forty, she didn't have a white hair on her head, and no wrinkles, except the tiny crow's-feet around her eyes which you wouldn't notice unless you were close and looked for them. "If I ever find a girl as pretty as you are," Hugh said, "I'm going to marry her. I keep looking, but I never find one."

"You go on now." She laughed, but she was pleased. "Hugh, we're leaving this place. You know how hard Pa's worked, and you've sent us money and Vic's helped us out, but we never have been able to get ahead. Pa always said that someday they'd build a railroad into this country and that the timber we own will be worth a fortune, but we've lived here fifteen years and there's no sign of a railroad. Your father's forty-nine and he had rheumatism last winter real bad. We can't live this way for another fifteen years, with our closest neighbor three miles away and the only doctor at Prineville — and he's so busy you can't get him if you need him."

She was talking in circles, afraid to come

to the point. Hugh asked, "Where are you going?"

She glanced at him and turned her gaze away quickly, frowning again. "We're going to Vic's ranch. He has a little house next to his big one. He needs someone who understands farming. His regular help are all cowboys and he has to hire some of the settlers to do the haying and all that. Pa's going to supervise the farming. He'll get a hundred dollars a month and the house to live in." She looked at him then. "Hugh, we haven't made twelve hundred any year since we were married. It just seemed like too good a chance to turn down."

Hugh nodded, keeping his face impassive against the feeling that boiled up in him. Hearn had been ding-donging at his folks to move over there for the last ten years, and Hugh wondered what had happened to change their minds.

One thing was certain. His mother didn't know Vic Hearn. Sure, they had been raised together. Hearn was an orphan, and her folks had taken him in when he was little; but she'd been married when she was sixteen and had left home. Hearn was her age. He might have been all right when he was a boy, Hugh had no way of knowing; but he knew what Hearn was now. It took a man to know, for Vic Hearn was the kind who could always fool a woman.

But he wasn't able to tell his mother. She had never let him say a word against Hearn. To her he was a brother, the only part of her family that was left, for both her parents had died, and she had been the only child. Besides, Hugh knew the move had gone too far to change. He said, "I see."

"It would have been different if you were home," she went on. "We always hoped you'd find a nice girl and get married and live here with us, but Vic says you'll never settle down, and I'm afraid he's right."

"Give me time," he said.

"You've had time," she said gently, and then dismissed the subject with a gesture. "Well, we're leaving in the morning. The wagon's loaded except for the trunk and suitcases, and a few things I left out in the kitchen."

"What's Pa doing in Prineville?"

"He's selling the horses. He's keeping Reddy, that sorrel gelding. You remember him. He's the best saddle horse we ever had. He's keeping the team of Percherons, too. He sold his cattle last week. There weren't many. We had a real bad winter, Hugh. We lost every one of the yearlings."

Always a bad winter, Hugh thought, or

lack of feed, or some disease. That's the way it had been from the day his father settled here. You couldn't lay it to laziness. Or cowardice. Hugh had never known a man with more physical courage than Sam Moberly. It wasn't stupidity, either. Just bad luck, year after year. If Hugh were superstitious, he would have said it was a jinx. All he knew was that he had met men like his father for whom nothing seemed to go just right. "Maybe it will be better working for Vic," Hugh said, but he knew it wouldn't. "Pa coming back tonight?"

"No, he'll meet us at Hamil's ranch tomorrow night."

"When did he leave?"

"This morning." She jumped up. "I've got supper on the stove. There's plenty and to spare."

He watched her cross the room, a graceful woman with a figure as trim as a girl's. She never worried. She never saw evil in other people. She never blamed her husband because he'd been a failure from the day they were married. Hugh shook his head. Failure wasn't the right word. Sam Moberly had loved and cherished her, and he'd made her happy. That, and that alone, raised him above the failure class.

Hugh rose and went outside. Vic Hearn

had wandered down to the river and was leaning against a pine tree, smoking a cigar. Hugh had told himself a moment before that his father wasn't stupid, yet he had been in this. He should never have left Hearn alone here overnight. But maybe it wasn't stupidity. Maybe it was faith. Or perhaps he didn't understand Hearn and what the man's motives were in making the offer he had.

Hearn took the cigar out of his mouth when Hugh came up. He said, "I reckon you know."

Hugh nodded. "She told me."

He rolled and lighted a cigarette. Hearn didn't have his hat on his head. His hair, as yellow as his heavy mustache, was worn a little too long. He could have been a Viking raider, Hugh thought, the kind who would have used his battle ax to cut a man in two, and he would have smiled all the time he was doing it, just as he was smiling at Hugh now.

"I think it will be better for both of them," Hearn said. "Of course, their home is your home if you're ready to settle down. I'll give you a job." His eyes became faintly speculative. "Except a gunslinging job, which is maybe all you know."

"In other words, you'd just as soon I kept moving?"

"I didn't say that," Hearn objected. "If you want to work, I'll give you a job. Let's leave it that way."

Hugh watched him walk toward the house, his back as straight as the barrel of a rifle. Suddenly Hugh realized that his own hands were clenched at his sides, and that the muscles of his forearms were drawn tight. In his indirect way, Hearn had made it clear that he didn't want Hugh around.

Hugh thought: *He's a damned stud horse. Why didn't I tell him if he ever laid a hand on Ma, I'd kill him?*

He knew at once why he hadn't. It wouldn't have done any good.

Chapter 2

Sam Moberly arrived in Prineville with his horses in late afternoon, and after a certain amount of haggling sold them to a livery stable for ten dollars less than they were worth. He would have done better if he had started looking for a market a month ago. He might have taken them to The Dalles, or across the Santiam Pass to the Willamette Valley, but there had been no time. There never was any time when you dealt with Vic Hearn.

Sam stepped into Landy's Bar and had a drink, lingering over it as he passed the time of day with a couple of ranchers from up Ochoco Creek. It was the first drink he'd had since fall; it was the first time he'd been in Prineville, for that matter. Now, feeling the warmth of the whisky and the pleasant glow that came from good talk, he realized how much he had missed all this, isolated as he had been for so long on the Deschutes. His nearest neighbor was three miles away, a bachelor with a sour disposition who wanted only to be left alone.

Later he ate supper by himself in the restaurant next to Landy's and all the time he was telling himself that it would be better, once he and Clara reached Hearn's Valley. They wouldn't be alone there. They'd be living next to Vic's big house. There'd be ranch hands around, and Vic's housekeeper, a girl named Jean Phipps; and because they'd be less than ten miles from town Clara could drive in when she wanted to.

After he finished eating, he walked the streets until the sun went down and dusk flowed in and covered the valley of Crooked River where the town lay. Then it was dark, and because he found no one that he knew he turned toward the hotel and got a room. He was tired and plagued by a spell of melancholy, but because he wasn't sleepy he sat by the window and smoked his pipe.

He hated to leave the Deschutes. That was the whole truth, and there was no use denying it. He'd had his dreams, based on the sale of his timber when the railroad came, but after fifteen years the railroad had not come. He had simply seen beyond his time. He was a poor man with stock, but a competent farmer. The trouble was, the sandy soil along the Deschutes wasn't good farm land unless it was irrigated, and it took money to put in a ditch. Even if he had been able to raise a crop, he had no market. Well, he'd hang onto his place and keep the taxes paid. Somebody might wreck the house, but if he had to come back he could always build again. He'd try working for Vic, and if it didn't pan out his place on the Deschutes would still be there.

But would Clara come with him? Could he ask her to return to this loneliness, once she had known how it was to have company and enough money to buy everything she needed and not be dependent on what Hugh and Vic gave them? He couldn't. He knew that as surely as he knew the sun would rise in the morning. He was selling himself into captivity. He would never be his own man again.

When his pipe went out, he rose and looked at himself in the cracked mirror above the pine bureau. Not a very strong face. The wispy mustache didn't help. No, not a very strong face, and certainly not a handsome one.

He blew the lamp out and went to bed. He lay there, seeing the reflection of his face, made older than his years by the deep lines that creased it, and he thought of his wife's face, beautiful and serene. She deserved more than he had been able to give her. She deserved everything that Hearn could do for her, and that, Sam knew, was why he had agreed to go. Clara never complained, but he had failed her just as he had failed Hugh, who had left home when he was fifteen. He fell asleep at last, and when he woke at dawn he felt as if he had not slept at all.

He had breakfast in the hotel dining room. As he was finishing his coffee, Hank Boyer, a stage driver who was scheduled to take the northbound stage out in half an hour, came in and sat down across from him.

"Howdy, Sam," Boyer said. "You're up early."

"I've got some riding to do today," Sam said. "Figured I might as well get started."

After the waitress took Boyer's order, he said, "I hear you're leaving the country."

Sam nodded. "I'm going to work for Vic Hearn in Hearn's Valley."

"I guess he's got a big outfit." Boyer leaned back in his chair, his weathered face speculative. "What do you aim to do with your place, Sam?"

"Keep it."

"Hell, man, you can't do that and work in

21

Hearn's Valley. It's too far from here."

"I know," Sam said, "but I'll keep it just the same."

"You'd be better off to sell it," Boyer said. "You don't even have a neighbor close enough to look after it. Some saddle bum will spend a night in your house and maybe burn it down. You'd better get something out of it when you can."

"You wouldn't be in the market, would you, Hank?"

Boyer squirmed around in his seat, then said, "I might. I like to go fishing on the Deschutes and I wouldn't mind having your place. It gets pretty damned cold over there if you have to camp out."

"Make me an offer," Sam said.

Boyer scratched his head. "I'll give you five hundred dollars cash."

Sam laughed and got up. "Five hundred dollars for the best timberland on the river! You'd have a good deal if you could get it for that."

"Wait." Boyer threw out a hand. "I had to start somewhere. What do you think your place is worth?"

"I don't know, but I'll keep it. Wouldn't surprise me if you knew a railroad was coming in this year. If it does, I've got a fortune over there."

Boyer grinned wryly. "You can't blame a man for trying, Sam. I don't know when a railroad's coming up the Deschutes, but I seen a survey crew working this side of the Columbia the last trip I made. If they ever do lay steel into this country, I'm out of a job."

"Maybe you can buy some other man's timber," Sam said. "It won't be mine. That's sure."

He nodded at Boyer and left the dining room. He saddled Reddy, and rode out of town with the sun barely showing above the Blue Mountains to the east. The air was very cold for an hour or more, then the sun cut away the chill, and after that the day was pleasant. Spring always came earlier on Crooked River than on the Deschutes.

He followed the river for several miles, then crossed it and went due south, taking a road that was hardly more than two wheel ruts across the hills. At noon he stopped beside a small stream, ate the sandwiches he had brought from the hotel, and, because there was no hurry, lay down under a juniper for an hour, his hat over his face.

The talk with Boyer had bothered him all morning. Rumors of railroad building had been prevalent for years, but so far they had been only rumors. Now, if Boyer had actually seen a survey crew south of the Columbia, there must be more to it than rumor. Sam was convinced Boyer wasn't lying; if Hank had been, he wouldn't have made an offer to buy, even for the ridiculous price of five hundred dollars.

But now that Sam had finally made the decision and had sold his stock, there could be no turning back. He'd made a wrong choice, he thought bitterly, and found himself plagued by doubts. He lay there, his eyes closed, remembering how it had been when he was first married. He'd been twenty-five and Clara sixteen — too much difference in age, her folks had said.

Vic Hearn had been sixteen, too, a gangling boy whose big-boned frame had carried the promise of the size he later attained. On the day before the wedding, Vic had taken him aside and told him not to marry Clara; but when he had said nothing would stop him, Vic had tried to whip him, and instead had taken a whipping himself.

Fighting and beating a sixteen-year-old boy had brought no glory to Sam and he had always been ashamed of it, but he'd had no choice. After that, Vic hadn't spoken to him until long after he'd left the country with Clara.

He hadn't done right by Clara, although

he'd tried hard enough. Her folks had been pretty well fixed, at least for a farming country like western Oregon, and they had been bitter about her marrying Sam, who had nothing. After the wedding, he took her south to the Rogue River Valley where Hugh was born. Later they moved to the coast, but Sam had barely made a living.

Though Clara wrote to her folks, she never heard from them. Neither Clara nor Sam understood, for she was an only child; although her parents had opposed the marriage, they had not been bitter enough to cut off all communication with her. Clara kept saying she should go home, but time passed and no word came from them. She just never got around to going. Sam knew how it was. If Clara had just received one letter . . . But because she hadn't, she felt rejected. If they didn't need her, she didn't need them. The result was that she lived for Sam and little Hugh.

When Hugh was eight, Sam lost his job in a sawmill where he had been working in Marshfield. Tired of the damp coastal climate, they returned to the Willamette Valley; and because Sam insisted on it they stopped at Clara's old home, only to find that her folks were dead, the farm sold, and no sign of Vic Hearn. None of the neighbors knew where he had gone.

The days after that were bitter ones. Clara blamed herself for staying away so long, for letting what she called her willful pride keep her away. Because she couldn't bear to live in the Willamette Valley, they crossed the Cascade Mountains and settled on the Deschutes River, an absolute wilderness at the time.

They had made a living, not a good one, but a living. Because there was no school for Hugh closer than Prineville, Clara had taught him, and she'd done a good job. Now, after all this time, Sam still did not know why Hugh had left home when he was fifteen. They had always got along together and Hugh had been a willing worker. Maybe it was just that the boy had seen no future at home.

In any case, Sam had not tried to make him stay. Neither had Clara. They'd given him a horse, a gun, and a little money, and he'd ridden off. He'd written from time to time; he usually came home once or twice a year, and he sent money home. No, there had never been anything wrong in their relationship with him. They had loved him and he had loved them, but they'd missed him more than they'd ever let him know.

Sam had never forgotten the day they'd

heard about Vic from a cowboy who had drifted by and stopped for a night with them, about the great Vic Hearn who lived in Hearn's Valley on his big H ranch and the little nearby town of Hearn City. He had driven a herd north from California when he was young, not over twenty-one or two, and had become rich.

Not that Vic's wealth was important to Clara. It was just that Clara had finally found the only living person she could consider a relative. She wrote to him, and within the month he rode in, surprising them. Clara recognized him before he stepped out of the saddle.

After that, Vic visited them at least once a year, always giving Clara money and always trying to get them to leave the Deschutes and live with him. He had been friendly enough to Sam, never mentioning the fight they'd had the day before Sam and Clara were married. Still, there had been a barrier between them which had grown wider with the years because Vic made barbed remarks about the way Sam and Clara lived, and reminded them of how well he had done. Because Clara was so happy, now that she had found Vic, Sam went out of his way to get along with the man, without letting Clara know how he felt.

Time to go, Sam thought, and got up and stretched. He wanted to reach Hamil's ranch before dark, yet he shrank from meeting Clara and Vic there. It meant the end of his old life, the beginning of a new one that he hoped would satisfy Clara, but one that he knew would never be right for him.

If Hugh would settle down and send for them . . . No, that wouldn't do, either, for Hugh had a right to his life, living the way he wanted to live. Vic had told Sam that Hugh was a paid killer, an outlaw with a price on his head. Though Sam didn't believe it, Vic acted as if he knew, and Sam wondered. Sam thought that it was part of Vic's plan to separate him from his son. He noticed that Vic never mentioned Hugh to Clara, and for that, at least, Sam was thankful.

After he left the creek, the land flattened out and he rode all afternoon through sage and rabbit brush, with an occasional juniper twisted into an odd shape by the wind that always seemed to blow on the high desert. When he reached Hamil's ranch at dusk, and saw the covered wagon, he knew that Vic and Clara had arrived before him.

As he stepped down, Clara saw him and ran to him, hugging him as if he had been gone for weeks instead of two days and a night. Now that he thought about it, he realized it was the longest time they had been separated since they were married.

He nodded at Vic, who stood on the other side of the campfire; then he saw Hugh coming toward him, and he called out, "Hugh!" thinking that he must be dreaming, and that this could not really be Hugh. Like Clara, he had been afraid they'd lose track of him when they moved.

"It's me, all right," Hugh said. "How are you, Pa?"

As they shook hands, Sam looked up at his son, and was comforted by the thought that he had sired a man.

Chapter 3

Hugh had no chance to talk to his father that night, for Vic Hearn was always around. Purposely so, Hugh thought, for Hearn certainly knew that Hugh did not approve of the move. Perhaps he thought that Hugh would persuade his father to go back, and that there would be less chance of success if more miles were put between them and the Deschutes.

They left Hamil's ranch at sunup, traveling east, the road following a long valley with rimrock to the north and rolling hills to the south. Although it was the first day of June, the morning was cold. Clara Moberly wore her coat and a scarf until almost noon. The only clouds in the sky were those swirling around the peaks of the Cascades to the west.

Hugh noticed that his father did not look back once during the morning. He remembered how often Sam had stood for minutes at a time staring at those peaks: the Three

Sisters, Broken Top, Bachelor, and the rest. It was almost as if he worshiped them, as if he could stand there beside the Deschutes River, which headed in that high country, and, by looking at the mountains, gain strength and faith from them, perhaps hope. He was a man, Hugh knew, who had never been able to find those sustaining qualities within himself. Now, with his mother driving the wagon, and Hearn riding beside him on the right, Hugh glanced at his father, who rode on his left. He had a sad face, Hugh thought, which with its deep lines and the fringe of white hair showing below his hatbrim seemed far older than it was. If he ever turned his head and looked at the mountains, he would swing around and ride back to the home he had left, Hugh told himself.

Although Vic Hearn was only nine years younger than Sam Moberly, he looked as if there was a generation between them. He might have been Sam's son, a man who had all the strength and vitality of youth and had known only victory, a man who had never become acquainted with doubt and therefore had no need to look at a mountain.

Hugh stared at the long sage-covered slope ahead of them that tipped upward toward the horizon, but he wasn't seeing it;

he wasn't seeing anything except disaster and final defeat for Sam Moberly.

After they nooned at the base of the rimrock to their left where they were out of the biting wind that swept across the high desert, they were on the move again, topping the ridge and starting down the long slope into a valley identical to the one they had left. Southward the juniper forest made a solid green mass against the sky.

Hearn dropped back to ride beside the wagon, giving Hugh a chance to ask the question that had been in his mind from the moment he had learned about the move. He asked, "Why did you do it, Pa?"

Sam glanced briefly at him and looked away. "Do what?"

"You know what I mean. Why are you leaving your own place?"

"Vic's made us a good offer," Sam answered, staring straight ahead. "We're to have a nice house and I'm to get —"

"I know," Hugh said impatiently. "Ma told me that, but I want to know why."

"We lost most of our cattle last —"

"Pa, you've got no need to beat around the bush with me. The place you left was your home. You lived there fifteen years. You own the best piece of timberland on the Deschutes, and you used to talk about a railroad. Well, I spent some time in The Dalles, and I came on south through Moro and Shaniko, and I heard the talk. The railroad's coming, all right. Maybe not tomorrow, but soon. So why did you leave now?"

Sam chewed on his lower lip a moment, then said slowly, "I guess my reason wouldn't make much sense to you. I'm sorry for one thing. It was the only home you ever knew. I always felt that you liked to come back to it."

"That's right, I did," Hugh said. "I've covered a chunk of ground in the last eight years, and I've done a lot of things. Some good and maybe some bad, but in the back of my mind was always the notion that someday I'd settle down beside you. There's plenty more good timberland. I've thought of getting a town going somewhere on the river." He laughed. "Just dreaming."

"It's a good dream," Sam said gravely. "I've thought of it, too. There'll be a town somewhere on the river, and not far from our place, I figure."

"You still haven't told me why."

"It was the loneliness, I guess," Sam said, "and I got tired of waiting. It was hard on your mother. I wanted her to have something better and I couldn't give it to her. Vic

33

can." He paused, then added dutifully, "He's like a brother."

He doesn't know, Hugh thought. *He doesn't know what Vic Hearn is, and it's too late now to tell him. He wouldn't believe me if I did.*

Presently Sam said, "You've asked me a question, so maybe I can ask you one. Vic hasn't told your mother, but he's told me that you've killed a lot of men and you've got a price on your head. Is it true?"

Hugh couldn't answer for a moment. He seldom felt a passionate hatred for anyone, the kind of hatred that made him want to kill a man. Yet now he found himself wanting to kill Vic Hearn, and suddenly he knew that someday he would. Finally he said, "I guess this is something you won't understand, either. Hearn's partly right. Just partly. I've hired my gun, but I've never done anything I'm ashamed of and I'm not wanted by the law."

Sam nodded as if he understood; but Hugh knew he didn't. After a time Sam said, "I've never seen you wear a gun."

"There was no reason to wear it when I came home," Hugh said. "It's tied up in my slicker back of the saddle. I'll leave it there until I need it — and I think that's going to be soon."

Sam glanced at him worriedly, asking, "You going to work for Vic?"

"Maybe. I haven't decided."

There was no more talk after that, for Hearn left the wagon and rode beside them as he had all morning. Hugh had said enough. There was no point in telling his father that he planned to stay in Hearn's Valley because his parents would need him as they had never needed him before.

It was a strange thing when he stopped to think about it. He couldn't actually put into words why he felt about Vic Hearn the way he did. He only knew that the feeling went back to his boyhood, to the very first visit Hearn had made. He had brought Hugh presents, and had tried to hold Hugh on his lap and talk to him; but Hugh remembered how he'd got a crazy wildness in him that made him squirm around and break free and run out of the house as soon as he could.

Looking back, Hugh could think of nothing tangible that had made him hate Hearn except a vague notion that the man was dishonest, that he was false. After Hugh left home, he'd heard enough about Hearn and his H ranch to know he was right. He would have told his folks if he'd had the slightest inkling that they planned a move like this.

Probably they wouldn't have believed him if he had told them. His mother had always been very sharp with him whenever he hinted that Vic Hearn was anything but a fine and upright man. Still, he would have tried if he had known; so in a way he was to blame for not going home more often, or at least keeping in closer touch with them.

After that, he said nothing more to his father about leaving the Deschutes. On the afternoon of the fourth day they reached the rim above Hearn's Valley. They drew up, Hearn turning to Hugh's mother and pointing to the valley that stretched for miles below them.

"Hearn's Valley," he said with pride. "That bunch of buildings you see is Hearn City. We'll sleep there tonight in the hotel and go on to H Ranch in the morning. It's on the other side under the rim."

"It's wonderful what you've done," Hugh's mother said. "You must be one of the richest men in the state."

"I suppose I am," Hearn said, "but not when the price of beef goes down." He glanced at Sam, showing his white, wide teeth in a smile and somehow contriving to exclude Hugh. "You always wanted a railroad. Well, it's different with me. I've done everything I can to hold a railroad back. I

36

don't want it. All it would do is to bring farmers to my valley. My money is cattle, and cattle walk to the railroad. See the difference, Sam?"

"Sure," Sam said. "Timber doesn't walk, and that's all the wealth I have."

"The valley's green," Hugh said. "There must be water."

"Plenty of it. Hearn's Creek heads yonder in the Blue Mountains." Hearn pointed to the long, undulating line of pine-covered ridges to the north. "It floods the valley every spring, so we always have a hay crop."

"But if there was a railroad," Hugh said, "ten times as many people could make a living in your valley as you have down there now."

"That's exactly what I don't want," Hearn said tolerantly, as if he were explaining something to a stupid child. "The people who live down there are farmers who raise hay for me, or for horses or mules. Some of 'em are freighters who haul supplies in from The Dalles. I don't let anybody have cattle because there's just enough grass for H cattle. Well, we'd best move along. It's quite a ways to town." He stepped out of the saddle and handed the reins to Sam. "I'll drive the wagon down. It's pretty steep."

Hearn climbed to the seat and took the lines from Clara. He asked, "Tired?"

"Pretty tired," she admitted. "I'll be glad to get there."

"You'll have a real bed tonight in the hotel," Hearn said. "Tomorrow we'll be home."

Home! Hugh looked at his mother, who brightened at the word. She had her hopes so high, he thought as he put his horse down the narrow road that was a sharp-pitched, narrow gash along the side of the cliff. But home was on the other side of the high desert, and she had gone off and left it.

He reached the valley floor and struck off across it toward town, green meadows stretching for miles on both sides of him. His father caught up with him, leading Hearn's horse, the heavy wagon rumbling down the grade behind them, brakes squealing. Neither of his parents would ever go back, for they had come here seeking happiness. Or was it the pot of gold at the end of the railroad?

As Hugh rode, the buildings of the town taking shape ahead of him, the burden of guilt became so heavy it was intolerable. He should have come home sooner.

Chapter 4

Hearn City consisted of a hotel, a saloon, a general store, a livery stable, and a dozen or more houses and shacks scattered haphazardly in the grass. A few of the dwellings were shaded by poplar trees, but most of them squatted in the center of bare yards, graceless and forlorn.

Vic Hearn drove the wagon alongside the west wall of the livery stable and stepped down, then held his arms up to Clara and swung her to the ground beside him. He said, "Sam, you and Clara go over to the hotel. Clara probably wants to rest before supper."

"I'd like to, Vic," Clara said. "Right now I don't think I could eat a bite."

"You'll feel better after you lie down a few minutes." Hearn walked to the back of the stable and called, "Daugherty." By the time the stableman came into view, Sam and Clara had disappeared in the direction of the hotel.

Hearn nodded at the team of Percherons. "Unhitch these horses and take care of them."

"Right away, Mr. Hearn," Daugherty said.

Hugh had not dismounted. Hearn looked at him, irritation showing in his face. "Get down, son," Hearn said. "Take care of the saddle horses."

Wheeling, Hearn strode across the road to the saloon. For a moment Hugh sat his saddle, staring at Hearn's broad back until the batwings of the saloon flapped shut behind him. He swung down and, untying the slicker behind the saddle, took out his gun belt and buckled it around him, then rolled the slicker up and tied it again, reflecting that this was the first time he could remember when Hearn's smiling, pleasant mask was marred by irritability.

Hugh led his horse and his father's sorrel to the water trough between the stable and the corrals behind it, leaving Hearn's mount ground-hitched. He slipped off the bridles and let the horses drink. When Daugherty finished with the Percherons, Hugh said, "You can take care of Hearn's animal."

Daugherty was a small man with weak eyes that blinked uncertainly as he looked at Hugh. He said, "Mr. Hearn likes to have folks do what he says."

"I figured that," Hugh said. "This is Hearn City in Hearn's Valley which ought to be called Hearn's Empire. That right."

"I dunno 'bout that," Daugherty said uneasily. "It's just that when he says . . ."

"The revolution is about to start," Hugh said. "His damned horse will stand there all night as far as I'm concerned."

He led his and his father's horse into the barn, found empty stalls, and tied them. He stripped gear from them, rubbed both animals down, and stepped back into the runway. He said, "A double bait of oats for both of them. I don't care what you do with Hearn's."

Hugh walked past the liveryman to the street, wondering if there was a free man in town. Or the valley, for that matter. In any case, Hugh wasn't the kind who would fit into this system of peonage. Because Hearn knew it too, he would find some way to get rid of him.

For a moment Hugh stood in the archway, the setting sun throwing long shadows against the gray dust of the street. Sooner or later he had to come to a decision. His alternatives seemed clear. He could ride on in the morning and pursue the same rootless life he had been following from the time he left home. He could stay, taking the job Hearn gave him, and submitting to the man's dominance as his father would. Or he could fight him.

He turned toward the hotel, deciding he had better ride on. He was not a man who could stay and submit. If he stayed, he would fight; he would kill Vic Hearn or be killed, and either way he would bring sorrow to his mother. He couldn't do that, yet he knew that grief would come to his mother no matter what he did. She had decreed it the moment she decided to come to Hearn's Valley, but if he stayed he would only make it worse.

At fifteen he had been too restless to stay at home. He did not regret leaving, but he'd had enough drifting, enough excitement, and when he'd reached The Dalles and heard the railroad talk he was ready to settle down. But his parents' decision had been made by the time he got home, so there was no reason to tell them what he had decided. Well, it was out of his hands now. He'd be on his way again in the morning, and they would never know how near he had been to doing what they had wanted for so long.

He found Hearn alone in the lobby. Hearn asked sharply, "You take care of my horse?"

Hugh understood what Daugherty meant

when he said that Hearn liked to have people do what he said; he understood the importance of the order and of his response to it. Rebels were not welcome in Hearn's Valley. The order had been a test, and Hugh had reacted in the only way he could.

"No," Hugh said. "Daugherty took care of him."

"I'm sorry you didn't do what I said." Hearn moved toward him, his gaze briefly touching the gun on Hugh's hip. "A man obeys me if he works for me."

"I'm not working for you yet." Hugh almost said he was leaving in the morning, then realized that this was not the time. He'd play it out, for a while at least. "I don't even know what kind of work you plan to give me, so I don't know whether I can do it. Or whether I want to."

"It won't be a gunfighter's job. I told you that."

"I remember. Like you said, maybe it's all I know."

"Then you won't do on H Ranch," Hearn said. "We'd better get something clear. You're not my blood nephew. I don't owe you a damned thing."

"I didn't figure you did. I never asked you for anything, either."

"I'll take care of your mother as long as

43

she lives. For her sake, I wanted to do what was right for you, but you don't make it easy."

"And Pa? You'll take care of him?"

"Sure."

He said it quickly and easily, as if there was no question about it. Hugh would have pressed it if his parents had not come down the stairs then. His mother had pinned up her hair and washed the desert dust from her hands and face. She seemed fresh and rested, but Sam, who followed her, looked desperately tired. The weariness of defeat, Hugh thought, and perhaps of regret.

"We're hungry," Clara said. "Are you, Vic?"

"Hungry enough to eat a horse." Hearn motioned toward the door that led into the dining room. "Let's see what they've got on the menu tonight." He laughed. "Not that it ever changes. Roast beef, steak, and ham. Chicken on Sunday. That's the size of it."

"And this isn't Sunday," Clara said as she led the way into the dining room.

The dining room was a small one, with only four tables covered by red-and-white checked oilcloth. Clara chose the one nearest to the window. Hearn held the chair for her, a small mark of courtesy that didn't occur to Sam. Hugh sat down across from

44

her, his father dropping wearily into the chair to his right. Hearn took the remaining chair, assuming his usual pleasant manner.

"They don't have much business," Hearn said. "I furnish the beef just to keep the dining room open, and they raise their own chickens. They have a storeroom where they keep ham and bacon and that sort of thing. A couple of farmers north of town raise hogs and cure the meat."

"Why do you need a dining room?" Clara asked.

"Partly for myself," Hearn said. "I want a place to eat when I'm in town. My buckaroos need it, too. On Saturday nights, anyway. Then there's the freighters and the stage drivers. We have a mail stage that comes in from Prineville twice a week and another one from Vale." He laughed. "The truth is, Clara, I choose the businesses that operate in my town, and I pick the people who run them. It saves me a lot of trouble in the long run."

"You own the valley?" Sam asked.

"All I need to," Hearn answered. "Owning land isn't so important, but owning all the means of transportation is. The stage lines are mine. The freighters who haul into the valley work for me. That's why I said I don't need a railroad."

A girl came out of the kitchen to take their orders, a slender blond girl not more than eighteen or twenty. She stood beside Hearn's chair, an order pad in her hand. Hugh glanced casually at her, then fixed his gaze intently on her, his attention sharpening. Though she was pretty, with a clear skin and regular features, there was something else about her that attracted him, an intangible that he couldn't put his finger on for a moment; then he decided it was a sweetness of expression he had seen in few women.

Hugh heard his mother give her order, then his father, and finally Hearn, and all the time he was looking at the girl so intently that he didn't understand the words the others said. Clara sat looking out of the window. Sam was slumped in his chair, too tired to hold himself upright.

Hearn's hand came up from his side to pat the waitress intimately, but she must have expected it, for she quickly stepped around the table toward Hugh, asking, "What will you have?" Hearn's hand continued to move upward to scratch the back of his neck, his expression unchanged.

"Steak," Hugh said; then he knew what it was he had vaguely sensed about the girl: independence of spirit, courage, a will to resist. She turned and walked toward the kitchen, moving quickly and gracefully. She had a good figure, her breasts pressing firmly against her blouse, her hips roundly curved, her ankles trim. Hugh glanced at Hearn. The man wanted her, he knew, wanted her so much it was a goading passion in him. Here was a girl, Hugh thought, that Hearn did not own.

He heard his mother ask, "What's her name, Vic?"

"Ellie Dunn."

"She's a good looking girl," Clara said.

Hearn nodded his agreement. "She's all right. She lives here with her father. He's bunged up so he can't do anything but odd jobs, like sweeping out and chopping wood. Actually, Ellie supports him."

Hugh thought, *I won't leave. If a girl can stand up against him, so can I.*

Chapter 5

Darkness had come by the time they finished supper. Hearn rose, saying, "I want to get an early start in the morning. I've got some business to attend to, then I'm going to bed."

"Me, too," Clara said, and Sam nodded.

But both lingered in the lobby after Hearn left the hotel, Sam dropping into a chair in the corner beside a sickly-looking geranium, and Clara standing in the doorway looking out into the street. They wanted to talk, Hugh thought, and he was curious about what was in their minds. This was the first time the three of them had been alone since he'd got back.

Sam filled his pipe, lit it, and puffed steadily on it, waiting for Clara to say something. Hugh walked to the door and stood beside his mother. A lighted lantern hung in the archway of the livery stable. Long panels of lamplight lay on the street from the saloon and the hotel, but there was no movement, no sound except the barking of a dog from some farm out on the grass.

An old man limped into the lobby from the rear of the hotel. He asked, "Everything all right, folks?"

"Just fine," Clara said, leaning against the door casing and smiling at him. "I was getting a little air before we went upstairs. I got terribly cold coming across the high desert, but it's very pleasant here."

"Summers are hot in the valley," the old man said, and limped into the dining room.

Hugh heard him clearing the table. Ellie Dunn's father, Hugh thought, and wondered how the old man had become crippled. Working for Vic Hearn, maybe. Like an old horse put out on pasture, he had been given a sort of pension by Hearn. But Hearn was letting Ellie run the hotel, and he'd said she was supporting her father. So it wasn't a pension at all. Not if Hugh had Vic Hearn sized up right. Probably the girl was the only reason he put up with her father.

"Hugh," Clara said.

The word broke his line of thinking. He said, "Yes?"

"You don't like Vic," his mother said. "You think we've done wrong coming here. Why?"

"You wouldn't believe anything I said

against him," Hugh told her. "I'd just make you mad, so I don't see any sense in talking about it."

Sam got up from his chair and walked to the door. "We've got a right to know why you don't like Vic. He's gone out of his way to do something for us. Don't seem right the way you treat him."

"What have I done?" Hugh demanded. "I've tried to get along with him."

"I know," Clara said. "You've tried, but he knows how you feel. I guess you can't be something you aren't. It shows in your voice and the expression on your face."

Hugh had not realized his feelings had been mirrored so clearly. Well, he had always known he wasn't a good actor.

"We've been hoping you'd settle down close to us so we'd see you more often," Sam said. "That's why we want you to work for Vic, but you can't work for a man you hate."

"No," Hugh said. "I can't. It isn't too late for you to go back, Pa."

"We can't do that," Clara said sharply, as if haunted by doubts she would not admit even to herself. "I've always felt guilty because I left home when I was married and never saw my parents again. Finding Vic after so many years made me feel better about it. I'm all he has, Hugh. I guess I want to make up for what I did when I left home."

"You don't owe him anything, Ma," Hugh said. "If you owe anything to anybody, it's to Pa. And me, though I guess I don't have any claim on you, going off the way I did."

"Of course you have a claim on me," Clara said. "You're our son and we love you. That's why we hoped you'd stay and work for Vic."

"You had to take a look at the other side of the hill," Sam said. "Now you've seen it, so it's time to come home."

"I'll try," Hugh said. "You go on to bed now. You're tired."

Clara nodded gravely. "I'm tired, all right, but I kind of hate to go to bed. It's the end of one thing and the beginning of another, and I guess I'm a little scared."

She had a right to be, Hugh thought. She knows she's done wrong and she's worried. He looked at his father, and knew it was worse with him. Sam Moberly had gone off and left his dream, and nothing would ever be quite the same again.

"I'll smoke a cigarette and go to bed," Hugh said, and stepped into the darkness.

He walked east along the road until he had gone past the last house, where he paused long enough to roll and light his cigarette, and then, turning, walked back slowly. His father had been right in saying he had to have a look at the other side of the hill. What was it that had made him leave home? He couldn't give any of the usual reasons. Now, thinking about it, he suddenly realized that in a way his situation was like his mother's when she married and left home, but there was a difference. She had never seen her parents again, but he hadn't cut his home ties. He'd been back several times; he had written; he had sent money home.

He reached the hotel and threw his cigarette into the street. When he went into the lobby, he found it empty, and it was only then that he realized he did not know what room he was to have. The dining room and kitchen were dark, but there was a lighted bracket lamp on the wall near the rear door at the end of the hall.

Somebody must be up or the lamp would have been blown out. The kitchen was on the right. Apparently bedrooms were on the left. Hugh walked along the hall, looking for a line of light under one of the doors, but he did not find one until he reached the last room.

He raised his fist to knock, then held it

motionless in mid-air. He heard Ellie say, "No, Mr. Hearn. Please!" And Hearn, "What do you think I let you have the hotel for? I've been waiting a hell of a long time for you to quit playing ring-around-the-rosy with me. Now I'm done."

Hugh turned away, telling himself this was no business of his. Ellie's father must be close by and he'd know what was going on. He was old and crippled, but there would be a gun in the hotel. Any father would have it handy when Hearn was around, and would use it at a time like this if Hearn's attention was distasteful to Ellie.

Maybe Hugh had been wrong in thinking the girl had courage and the will to resist; maybe he had seen something in her that he wanted to see but that had not been there at all. No doubt her resistance was just part of the game women had played with men from the beginning of time. But he had not gone three steps before he heard the sounds of a scuffle; then Ellie cried out and he heard Hearn curse and the solid *whack* of a blow.

Hugh whirled back to the door, drawing his gun as he turned. He gave the knob a twist and kicked the door open. Hearn stood in the middle of the room, blood dripping from long scratches on one side of his face. Ellie lay sprawled across the bed, a hand raised to her right cheek, her eyes glazed with terror.

Hearn swung around to face Hugh when he heard the door slam open, but he made no move toward his gun. Hugh said, "Well, by God, Vic, can you think of any reason why I shouldn't kill you where you stand?"

Hearn laughed, a genuine laugh that rolled up out of his belly. Hugh felt the push of that laugh as if it were a force propelling him out of the room. Fear was a normal emotion in a situation like this, yet Hugh was convinced that Vic Hearn would not be afraid of anything or anybody under any circumstances.

Ellie jumped up, calling out, "No, Mr. Moberly! No! It's all right. Let us alone."

Hearn asked, "Hear that, sonny?"

"You still haven't given me any reason why I shouldn't kill you," Hugh said.

"There's quite a few," Hearn said. "Ellie don't want you to, for one thing. Number two, you'd be hunted down and strung up in less'n twelve hours. Maybe those two don't count, but a third one will. How would you explain it to your mother?"

That one counted, all right. Hugh holstered his gun. Funny how that single question cooled his fury. This was something he had known from the moment they had left the Deschutes. He was helpless until his mother found out for herself what Vic Hearn really was.

"I told you it was all right, Mr. Moberly," Ellie said. "Will you let us alone, please?"

"He'll let you alone," Hearn said genially. "So will I. For tonight. I guess we gave each other something to think about." He rubbed a hand across his cheek; then Hugh, looking at the girl, saw the dark bruise below her left eye. "We'll talk about it again, Ellie. Come on, Hugh."

As Hearn walked toward the door, Hugh retreated into the hall. Hearn pulled the door shut, then stood looking at Hugh. His face was shadowed because the bracket lamp was behind him, but Hugh could make out the speculative expression he had seen on the big man's face before. Not doubt, but one of unexpected pleasure, as if he was facing a problem that challenged him.

"You know, son," Hearn said, "I haven't had a hairpin like you in the valley for quite a while. A couple of years ago we strung up a horse thief. When I first came here, a man insisted on keeping cows after I told him there wasn't room in the valley for anything but H cattle. He wound up with a slug in his brisket. But I ain't real sure about you yet.

There's been some big yarns about you that saddle tramps have fetched in. About the ruckus you were in on the Laramie. And on the Yampa in Colorado. If they're true, you're a tough nut. If they ain't, you'll slope along in a day or two and everybody will be a hell of a lot better off."

"They're probably not true," Hugh said. "I came back here to find out which room I'm supposed to have, and I still don't know."

"Ten," Hearn said. "At the head of the stairs. Well, we're honest men. You never have liked me, and I sure as hell don't like you. You were a spoiled pup when you were a kid. Too bad Clara didn't have ten brats. You wouldn't have ruled the roost like you did."

He laid a hand on Hugh's shoulder. "Let's go over and have a drink, then we'll go to bed. If you want to ride out to H Ranch in the morning, just to take a look, that'll be fine. There's a thousand dollars in it if you keep on riding."

"I think I'll take that job you offered me," Hugh said, "and I don't want a drink."

"You'll have one," Hearn said. "At least you'll walk over to the saloon with me. You see, a gunslinger drifted into town while I was gone. He's looking for you. Aims to kill you, he says."

56

"What's his name?"

"Smith. Jones. Brown." Hearn laughed. "How the hell would I know? I told him I figured you'd crawl out of town when you heard, but he said no, you were a game one, which I doubt."

"Why does he want to kill me?"

"You ran off with his sister. You slept with his wife. You shot his brother in the back. Maybe you kicked his dog. He never said." Hearn started along the hall toward the lobby. "Coming? Or are you as scared as I figure?"

"I'm coming," Hugh said, and followed Hearn across the lobby and into the street.

It was a put-up job, and Hearn knew that Hugh knew it. Killing the man would prove nothing; it would settle nothing. Hugh had come home intending to stay because he was tired of the life he had been living, tired of killing, tired of drifting. But the very life he had lived had set a standard for him. Now a compulsion was driving him to do something he didn't want to do at all.

Hearn, glancing back at him, knew Hugh would meet the man who was waiting for him in the saloon.

Chapter 6

Hugh found the saloon exactly as he expected it: a long pine bar on one side of the room, a couple of green-topped tables on the opposite side, and a swinging lamp overhead. A bald-headed man with the usual dirty apron tied over a bulging belly stood behind the bar, an uneasy expression on his moonlike face. The only other man in the saloon sat at the second table, his hat tipped down over his forehead, a deck of cards spread out before him.

"Let's have that drink, Hugh," Hearn said genially as they crossed to the bar. He nodded at the bartender. "My private bottle, Myers."

"Only the best, Vic," Hugh said.

The man playing solitaire straightened, his head snapping up when he heard Hugh's voice. He said, "Well, by God, ain't it funny what the wind blows in when you ain't looking?" Hugh whirled, not expecting the encounter so fast. His hand dropped to gun butt as the man at the table rose, the tension that an anticipated fight always brought to him suddenly breaking. The laugh was on Vic Hearn. The man at the table was Joe Pope, a gunman who had ridden with Hugh during the trouble on the Laramie.

It had been a bloody affair, with charges and countercharges of rustling and horse thieving, and threats of hanging on both sides. It had come close to being more than a threat for Pope. He had been caught by the others and would have been hanged if Hugh hadn't showed up at the right place and the right time and saved him.

"Just about as funny as what the wind blows in before you get to where you're going," Hugh shouted at Pope.

They charged across the saloon toward each other, hands extended. They pummeled each other good-naturedly while they exchanged insults, then Pope grabbed Hugh by the arm and propelled him toward the bar.

"I'll have a drink out of your private bottle, too, Mr. Hearn," Pope said. "This is the damnedest thing. I ain't seen this ugly son-of-a-bitching horse thief since we rode together on the Laramie."

"What grounds have you got for calling me ugly?" Hugh demanded. "And with a face like yours?"

"Plenty of grounds," Pope jeered. "I never broke no looking glass just by staring into it."

"And I never had a woman look at me and say, 'Give me the rear end of a bull. It's better looking than this hombre's mug.' Remember her, Joe?"

"I clean forgot about her." Pope laughed. "Hell, she wasn't no beauty, neither." He hammered the bar with his fist. "Come on, Myers. Where's that private bottle?"

The bartender had been standing motionless, his round face holding a strange mixture of relief and disappointment. Then he bent down, lifted a bottle from under the bar, and set it and three glasses in front of Hearn.

Hugh glanced at Hearn and wanted to laugh. He had never seen Vic Hearn visibly jarred before, for he was a man who kept himself under tight control just as he dominated every situation in which he found himself. But this one, for all of his planning, had completely escaped him. He stared at Pope, open-mouthed, then caught himself and, turning to the bar, picked up the bottle and filled the glasses. "This is an interesting accident, you two running into each other," Hearn said.

"Not such an accident," Pope said. "I

knew Ruth lived in Oregon, but I didn't know where. Fact is, I never been in this country till last fall." He rubbed the back of his neck, grinning ruefully. "I can still feel that damned rope." He turned to Hearn. "He saved my gizzard. It was the tightest squeeze I ever got into. By God, they had me on my horse with the rope on my neck when old Hugh here comes riding up with a gun in each fist. Them bastards took out of there like cowboys going home to dinner."

"Must have been a tight one," Hearn said. "Saw St. Peter waiting for you, I suppose."

"That's the truth, Mr. Hearn," Pope said. "He was standing right there in the pearly gate holding out his hand and saying, 'Hallelujah, Joe, come home to Papa.' "

Hearn lifted his glass, avoiding Hugh's gaze. "Drink up, boys. To a peaceful life here in Hearn's Valley."

They drank, Pope smacking his lips. He was a rough one, born to trouble, always seeking it, and enjoying his job because he was paid to do what he liked. Hugh had never been his close friend, but Joe had his own strange code that he would not violate even for money. The fact that they had once fought on the same side had not been important. Only one thing was. Hugh had

61

saved his life, and therefore Pope owed him a debt. But was it paid off now? Would it be different next time? Hugh didn't know.

Pope put his glass down. "Where you been, Hugh? When our outfit busted up, you rode south and I went north. Heard about you a couple of times since then. That's all."

"I was on the Yampa a while," Hugh said. "I had to get out of there in a hurry, so I spent the winter in Brown's Hole, then lit out for Utah. Headed for Idaho after that. Just came down from the Columbia the other day."

"Where you headed now?"

"Right here." Hugh glanced at Hearn, whose familiar smile was on his face again, one big hand palm down on the bar, the other at his side. "I'm going to work for Vic, I guess. My folks are moving out there, too."

"Yeah?" Pope glanced questioningly at Hearn, then brought his gaze to Hugh's face. He scratched his long nose, pale blue eyes narrowed as he seemed to be thinking about something that bothered him. "Your pa, maybe?"

"Pa and Ma both," Hugh said.

Pope was looking at Hearn again, but Hearn said nothing. Pope reached for the bottle, asking, "Want another drink of Mr. Hearn's good whisky, Hugh?"

"No, thanks," Hugh said. "You living here in the valley, Joe?"

Pope nodded. "Been here since last September. I'll see you again, Hugh. Lots of things to talk about."

Hugh knew it was time to go, but he lingered, wondering if Hearn would let it drop. "Sure are," Hugh said. "Remember the time you put a fistful of tacks in Slow Mike's bunk?"

Pope pounded the bar with his fist, and laughed. "I'll never forget it. You'd poured molasses into a bucket and shoved it under his bunk. You had a string tied to it and you pulled it out just as he hit the floor. He jammed a foot into the damned bucket and, by God, I thought he was gonna tear the bunkhouse down."

Hugh laughed. "He cussed for a week." He glanced at Hearn. He wouldn't do anything else tonight, Hugh thought. He said, "Well, so long, Joe."

Hugh walked out, leaving a sudden and disquieting silence behind him. Hearn would give Pope a cursing and maybe fire him. But Joe Pope was not a man who would take a cursing from anyone, and Hearn would know that.

As Hugh crossed the street to the hotel, he wondered how it would be the next time he met Pope. He could be sure of only one thing: Hearn would try again. Measured by cold logic, Hugh knew he was the worst kind of a fool for going out to H Ranch in the morning, yet that was exactly what he would do.

He dropped off to sleep as soon as he was in bed. He was wakened by a tap on his door. It was black dark, and he had no notion of the time. He had locked the door, but because the lock was a flimsy one he had jammed a chair under the knob. He took his gun from under his pillow as the tap came again, louder this time, and he heard Pope's voice, "Hugh! Let me in."

Hugh hesitated a moment, considering the possibility that Hearn had talked Pope into killing him regardless of what had happened in the past. Pope loved money, and if the price was high enough he might have agreed to it. Then Hugh knew he was wrong. This kind of killing was not Pope's way. Hugh removed the chair, turned the lock, and opened the door. As Pope slipped into the room, he said, "Keep your voice down. I damned near lost my job tonight. I never seen Hearn so mad. I'd still lose it if he knew I was talking to you now."

"Then you shouldn't be here."

"Aw, to hell with him." Pope sat down on the bed. "I'm a bastard, but by God, alongside Vic Hearn I'm a saint! You know what he aimed to do?"

Hugh sat down beside Pope. "Sure. You were supposed to prod me into a fight tonight and kill me."

"That was the last thing he figured out, but that wasn't what he had in his noggin when he left the valley a week or so ago. He said he'd be back with a man and a woman. He said the man was middle-aged and he wasn't no fighter. Hearn was gonna get him into the saloon and I was to kick him around until he either fought or crawled. Hearn said he'd give him his gun so it would look like he'd had a chance."

Hugh gripped Pope's arm. "He must have meant Pa."

"That's what I got to thinking after you left tonight. Hearn didn't say so. Started to cuss me out for not smoking you down, and I told him he had a good place for me to shove my gun barrel if he didn't shut up. He did, but when I asked him if I was fired he said no. So I'll stick around because the pay's good. Then I got to thinking 'bout your folks and decided I'd best tell you."

"Thanks, Joe." Hugh thought about what

Pope had said, then asked, "He told you to-night that you were taking on somebody else?"

"Yeah, soon as he got to town. Hell, I didn't know who it was. I didn't see you and he didn't give me no names." Pope paused, then said somberly, "It's a funny game, Hugh. You make your own rules and you play it that way. Trouble is, my rules don't jibe with Hearn's. That son of a bitch don't have none."

"No," Hugh said. "I figured he didn't."

"Take my advice and don't go to H Ranch in the morning," Pope said. "I dunno what he'll do now, but he'll figure another way of getting at you. Some of his buckaroos are all right, but he's got a foreman named Oscar Phipps who's bad medicine. And another fellow who calls himself Shagnasty Bob. He must be wanted somewhere, though I can't place the booger."

"I've got to go there," Hugh said.

"Then there's Phipps' daughter, Jean. She's Hearn's housekeeper and sleeps with him all the time. She's a real bitch, but she sure can get under a man's hide. I made a try, but hell, I wasn't big enough for her." Pope gave Hugh a sharp glance. "You always were a stubborn bastard."

Hugh nodded. "I guess I am."

"All right," Pope said. "It's your hide, but it's sure funny, watching a man light a shuck after his own hearse."

He left the room, pulling the door shut behind him. Hugh didn't go to sleep until nearly dawn. He lay awake, thinking how close his father had been to death. Or if he had crawled, he would have been worse off, for the last vestige of his self-respect would have been gone. But again he knew his father wouldn't believe him if he told him.

Chapter 7

Clara Moberly woke with the night blackness still in the room. For a moment she was bewildered and confused and a little frightened. She couldn't remember where she was or why she was here. She didn't even know what had wakened her. Then she heard a knock on the door, and was out of bed and halfway to the door before she realized where she was. Whoever was knocking must have been there quite a while, she thought, her mind still fuzzy from sleep. That was probably what had wakened her.

She opened the door a crack. "What is it?"

Hearn stood outside, fully dressed. He said, "Time we were going. Breakfast's about ready."

"We'll get dressed right away, Vic." She was fully awake now. "I'm sorry we weren't up. I guess I forgot to ask you when you wanted to start."

"It's all right," he said. "But hurry, will you?"

"We'll hurry," she said. Shutting the door, she turned to the bureau and fumbled around until she found the matches.

She lighted the lamp, then shook Sam awake. "Get up. Vic wants to start early."

He raised up on one elbow. "It's still night."

"I don't know what time it is, but Vic said breakfast was about ready."

Sam yawned and put his feet on the floor. He rubbed his eyes and yawned again. "What'd we go to bed for? Might as well have stayed up and driven out there last night."

Clara didn't say anything. It had been warm when they'd gone to bed, but it was cool now, and she shivered before she was fully dressed. She washed her hands and face, and brushed and pinned up her hair, feeling pride in it as she always did. It hung below her waist, solid black without a single white hair. She looked at herself for a moment in the wall mirror above the bureau, pleased with her appearance, confident that she didn't look forty. But Vic didn't, either.

Sam had been dressing slowly, yawning and grumbling about getting up in the middle of the night. Clara gave her hair a final pat, and turned to look at Sam. For some reason which she could not identify, she saw Sam differently than she ever had before. Strange she had never noticed it, but suddenly he looked older than he was. Perhaps it was because she had been thinking she and Vic looked younger than their years.

Sam rose and, walking to the bureau, emptied the basin into the slop jar and filled it again and washed. He was stooped, and there was no real authority in his motions or his voice when he said, "Reckon we'll have to get up early from now on."

If Sam had had more energy, Clara thought, they might not have suffered the winter loss that they had, even with the weather as bad as it had been. As Sam stood in front of the mirror running a comb through his white hair, she remembered how her parents and Vic had opposed her marriage, saying Sam was too old for her.

She assured herself it was not true. She and Sam loved each other. They'd had a good life together. She was ashamed of herself for thinking anything else. Yet, as they walked down the stairs, she was plagued by the thought that if Vic and Hugh had not given them money they would have been hungry many times in the years since Hugh left home. Hearn was waiting for them in the lobby. He said, "Good morning," his face grave.

"Good morning," Sam said, and yawned.

Clara saw the long scratches on Vic's cheeks, and asked, "What happened?"

"Happened?" He frowned, then put a hand to the side of his face. "Oh, you mean them scratches? Just a cat. I've kept her around the hotel too long." He motioned toward the dining room. "Ellie's got breakfast ready."

"Isn't Hugh up?" Sam asked.

"No, I figured we'd let him sleep. He was up pretty late last night." He motioned toward the saloon. "Celebrating. He'll get out there by the time we do anyhow."

They went into the dining room and sat down, Clara trying to keep from being upset by the knowledge that Hugh had been drinking the night before. She realized she had not really known Hugh since he was fifteen. She had seen him only at his best when he had visited for a few days and when there were no saloons closer than Prineville.

She ate her oatmeal and coffee, her head bowed, trying to defend Hugh in her mind by arguing that he was young and had a right to drink if he wanted to. All he needed was a little more time and he'd settle down, but her reasoning wouldn't quite satisfy her.

71

She'd had so many hopes for him when he was younger, so many fine dreams; but none of them would work out. Well, it showed how foolish she was, as foolish as Sam, who had talked all these years about a railroad coming, and selling their timber and being rich.

She didn't really notice Ellie until the girl brought a plate of biscuits and a dish of apple butter to the table, then, glancing up, she saw how glum Ellie was. When the girl returned to the kitchen, Clara asked, "What's the matter with her?"

"I don't know," Hearn said. "What makes you think something is the matter?"

"She was pleasant last night, but she's awfully sour this morning."

Hearn shrugged. "Sleepy, maybe. Or had a fight with her beau." He rose. "Let's get hooked up, Sam. We'll be ten minutes or more, Clara, if you want another cup of coffee."

"I think I would," she said.

After they left, Ellie brought the coffeepot and filled Clara's cup. She lingered at the table as if wanting to say something, and Clara, glancing at her, had the feeling that here was a pretty girl who had lost her capacity for seeing beauty in anything. Clara wondered about the bruise below Ellie's eye, but she wasn't going to ask about it. "Is there anything I can do for you?" Clara said.

She felt foolish as soon as she asked the question. It was just that she had always wanted to help people and there never was anyone she could help. Except Sam. And now Vic. But not Hugh. He had been gone so long. Besides, he made her feel he didn't need help of any kind. He was big and strong and capable. She couldn't understand how her boy could be the man Hugh was. Her mind was wandering and she brought it back sharply, her eyes on Ellie, who stood motionless beside the table, the coffeepot in her hands.

Ellie acted as if she hadn't heard Clara's question, but she had, for finally she said, "No, there's nothing you can do." She started to turn away, then swung back. "Mrs. Moberly, you and your husband are going to live with Mr. Hearn on H Ranch?"

"Yes. My husband is going to supervise his farming. Vic's my brother, you know."

"No, I didn't know," Ellie said. "You don't look alike."

Clara smiled. "Well, he isn't my blood brother. I grew up with him. You see, my folks raised him, then I lost track of him after I was married. When I found out where he lived, I wrote to him and he came to see us. It was wonderful to find him after so long."

Ellie nodded, started to turn away, and again turned back. "I'm not really a busybody, but I'm going to be one now. Mr. Hearn has a housekeeper named Jean Phipps. Watch out for her, Mrs. Moberly. She's mean."

"But I won't . . ."

Ellie didn't wait to hear what Clara started to say. She turned and this time walked away, quickly. Clara finished her coffee and went upstairs to get the few things she had brought from the wagon, and all the time she was wondering why Ellie had said that.

Maybe the girl was a busybody, even though she denied being one. But whether she was or not, why should she think there could be any trouble with a housekeeper? She'd ask Vic. No, she'd better not. It would just get Ellie into trouble, and Clara sensed that Ellie was in enough trouble now.

By the time she returned to the lobby, the wagon was in front of the hotel, gray light creeping over the valley. She climbed to the seat, taking the lines from Hearn, who handed them up to her. They started out, going directly east from town.

The last of a long journey, she thought with relief. It would be nice to settle down again, to be around other people. She wished Ellie hadn't said what she had about Jean Phipps, for it marred the perfect picture which had been in Clara's mind.

The sky above the eastern rim burned with a bright scarlet flame, then the sun came up, and it was full day. An hour from town they reached the creek, which was high, washing over the road on both sides of the bridge. The mud was deep, and the Percherons, strong as they were, had to be rested often.

Hearn dropped back and rode beside the wagon, giving her directions. Once he said apologetically, "It isn't like this most of the year, Clara. Just when the creek's high. But it's what gives me a good ranch." He pointed below the bridge where the water spilled out over the floor of the valley, making a huge, shallow lake. "That's our best hay land, even if it looks like a frog pond now. It's natural irrigation, and therefore the cheapest."

It seemed to Clara that they took a long time to get out of the mud and onto the higher, dusty land. After that, they moved faster, but it was well into the morning before they covered the ten miles to the ranch. She studied the buildings a long time before they arrived, and pride took possession of her.

She had never seen a truly big ranch before. She was proud because she and Sam would be a part of this, and because it was Vic Hearn's ranch, a ranch which he had started and built and which had made him the richest man in this part of the state. One of the richest in the whole state, she guessed.

H Ranch was as large as a good-sized town. There was the big white house, two stories, standing close to the rim and up on a slope so that it looked out over the entire valley. A long row of slender poplars made a green line in front of it. A small white house stood to Clara's left. Hers and Sam's, she thought.

The houses and their small outbuildings were above the road, and on the lower side were a huge circular barn, the cook shack, the bunkhouse, and a number of sheds. On below the barn Clara saw a maze of stockade corrals. Beyond were the hayfields, and on the other side of the valley, far to the west, Clara could see the rim they had descended yesterday afternoon. In spite of the distance, the rim was a straight line that stood out clear and sharp against the cloudless sky, the sunlight so brilliant it was almost blinding.

When Vic reached the small house, he motioned for Clara to draw up in front of it. He dismounted and stood waiting by the door. When she stopped, he held up his arms to her and helped her down, and even when her feet were on the ground, he still held her solidly around the waist, smiling down at her, as genial and pleasant as she had known him from the first day he'd ridden up to their log house on the Deschutes. Sam swung out of the saddle and walked toward them, then stopped and stood there, indecisive and hesitant as he watched Hearn.

"You're home, Clara," Hearn said. "I've looked forward to this for a long time. Let's see, it was twenty-four years ago that you left."

"It's been a long time, Vic," she said.

He let her go, wheeling toward Sam. "Unhook and take the horses to the barn. I'll have somebody come up and help you unload the wagon." He turned back to Clara. "You and Sam will have supper with me tonight. Jean's probably stocked your pantry with grub. If she hasn't, come over and get anything you need."

He stepped back into the saddle and then,

leading Sam's sorrel, rode toward the barn. Clara walked up the path to the house. It was clean and pleasant outside, with green grass between the front door and the poplars. Hearn's big house was not far away. She'd see him every day. She had no worry now about Sam's future and hers. If only Hugh would stay, too.

A woman appeared in the doorway, young, probably not over twenty. She was not as pretty as Ellie Dunn, but attractive enough, with full red lips and high cheekbones and the darkest blue eyes Clara had ever seen.

"You must be Jean Phipps," Clara said. "I'm Clara Moberly, Vic's sister."

"I know all about it, Mrs. Moberly," the woman said, "and I know all about you. You're not Vic's sister at all, and your husband's an old man who won't live long. Let's get one thing straight. Vic belongs to me, and don't you forget it for a minute!"

Jean walked past Clara and went on toward the big house. Clara stood looking at her until she disappeared, all the joy going out of this moment that she had anticipated for so long. She knew now what Ellie had meant when she'd said Jean Phipps was mean.

Chapter 8

When Hugh went downstairs, he found Ellie waiting for him in the lobby. She said, "Your folks went on out to the ranch. I'll get your breakfast right away."

She started toward the dining-room door, but he grabbed her arm and turned her back to face him. He asked, "Why didn't somebody wake me? Didn't Hearn —"

"I don't know the answer to any of your questions, Mr. Moberly." Ellie tried to jerk free. "Mr. Hearn never tells me why he does things."

"Looks to me like Ma or Pa would have got me up." He was angry with them, and angry with himself for not waking up; then Hugh thought bleakly there was no limit to what Hearn would do, no limits to the lies he would tell to try to separate him from his parents. Hugh was still holding Ellie by the arm, looking at her but actually not seeing her; then he released her, ashamed of having dragged his troubles into the open in front of her. For a moment she stood motionless, looking at him as if measuring him. He saw the purple bruise below her eye; but, more important, he perceived the grimness which was so evident in her.

She whirled away as if not wanting to expose her troubles to him any more than he wanted to parade his before her. "I'll get your breakfast," she said as she hurried into the dining room.

He caught up with her. "Where was your father last night?"

"You butted in once. That ought to be enough to satisfy you."

She pushed open the swinging door into the kitchen and went on. He followed her, catching the door as it started back toward him. "Do you know what would have happened to you if I hadn't butted in?"

She walked to the stove and moved a frying pan from the back of the range to the front, asking, "Will ham and eggs be all right?"

"Sure. I asked you if you —"

"If you'll wait in the dining room, I'll bring your breakfast to you. We don't allow customers in the kitchen."

"I'm special." He sat down in a chair at the table. "I like the smell of frying ham."

She whirled to face him, hands on her

hips, two bright spots of color appearing in her cheeks. She said furiously, "There is nothing you can do for me or my father or your folks, but there is something you can do for yourself. Ride out of the valley as soon as you finish breakfast."

She turned back to the stove. Silence then, broken only by the sizzling of ham in the frying pan and the metallic ticking of the clock on a shelf beside the stove. He looked at her back, held rigidly stiff, and he sensed the misery and shame that was in her because of what had happened last night. Fear, too, perhaps, for what would happen in the future.

"Ellie," he said gently, "I'm not riding out after breakfast. For a while I thought I would, but I can't. Would you like to know why I changed my mind?"

She didn't answer. She forked ham from the frying pan into a plate and broke two eggs into the grease. He went on, "I'll tell you, anyway. I saw Hearn look at you when you came to take our order last night. I knew what he was thinking about. It's probably what he thinks about every time he sees a pretty girl. But I saw something else that was more important. You were fighting him. I thought that if you had that much courage, I'd better find some, too."

She gave him a quick glance, blinking hard, then looked at the frying eggs. She said, "I've been fighting him for a long time, but I don't know whether I have the courage to keep on fighting him or not. There are some other women in the valley who haven't." She cleared her throat, then added, "He's a strange and powerful man, Mr. Moberly, the kind women first hate and then love."

"You love him? Or think you will?"

"No, I'm not like other women. I'll always hate him. I think I'll kill him someday."

She spooned the eggs into the plate, picked up the coffeepot, and walked past Hugh into the dining room. A moment later she returned, took biscuits from the warming oven, and walked back to the door. "Your breakfast will get cold if you don't come and eat it, Mr. Moberly."

"Hugh," he said.

"All right, Hugh," she said. "Will you . . . please come and eat your breakfast?"

"If you'll sit down and talk."

"You're a stubborn man." She sighed and sat down at the table. "I wonder how long your stubbornness will let you live."

"I've wondered, too," he said. "Now let's . . ."

"I'll answer your questions. I know what would have happened to me last night if you hadn't butted in. If it had, I would have killed him. I'm sure of that." She stared down at her hands folded on her lap. "You asked about my father. He's an old man and he's crippled. There was nothing he could do."

Hugh stopped eating long enough to say, "He must have a gun."

She nodded. "And I've asked him not to use it. I told him I could take care of myself. I have been able to until last night. He's never laid a hand on me before."

Hugh continued to eat, not knowing what to say. He understood Vic Hearn better than Ellie Dunn. For a man like him, the pleasure was in the pursuit and the conquest, but once the conquest was made the pleasure was gone.

"It's not a good world," the girl said after a moment of silence. "Not for me or my father. Maybe it is for you because you're strong. You shape life to suit you. That's what Hearn does, but I can't do it. Neither can my father." She leaned forward, her gaze on Hugh's face. "We have enough money to buy a stage ticket to Prineville. Or Ontario if we want to go that way. But what would we do then? Do you know what it is to be broke, Mr. Moberly?"

"Hugh," he said.

"Well, do you? So broke you don't know where your next meal is coming from? Or where you'll sleep or what you'll wear if your clothes wear out? We do, and it isn't a nice feeling."

She lowered her gaze, a hand coming up to rub her forehead. "Hearn has been kind to us in his way. He gave my father work until Pa fell off the roof of the barn on H Ranch and broke his leg. The people who had been running the hotel walked off and left it, so Hearn turned it over to us. It's a living, Hugh. Not much of a living, but we don't go hungry and we have a place to sleep, and so far we've made enough to buy the clothes we need."

He leaned back in his chair, rolled and lighted a cigarette. He knew what it was to be hungry, all right, but he didn't have an old and crippled father to look after. No, he had never been in Ellie's position. There was no escape for her, and he was sure that was exactly the way it seemed to her.

"You're a brave woman," he said.

"Not brave," she protested. "Desperate and scared, but not brave." She shook her head at him. "You can't do any good by staying. I said you were a strong man, but you're not strong enough to whip Vic Hearn. What good will it do if you get yourself killed?"

"None, maybe, but I've got to stay in the valley."

"Because of your folks?"

He nodded, then asked, "What about the other women you mentioned?"

"There have been several, but they're all gone except one. It's his housekeeper, Jean Phipps. I think she hated him once, but she doesn't now." She looked away from him, frowning. "Your mother is a fine-looking woman, Hugh, but your father doesn't have your strength. What will happen?"

"I guess we both know," Hugh said bitterly. "That's why I've got to stay. What kind of a man would I be if I rode away?"

"Not the man you are," she said. "I knew that, I guess. So you'll die. That's the way it has been with everyone who tried to stand against Vic Hearn. The strong die or leave because there's nothing here that seems worth fighting for. Only the weak stay."

He could not doubt the truth of what she said, but it did not change anything for him. If he stood alone, he had no chance, but there must be some who had as much courage as Ellie Dunn. He rose, asking, "Is there a man in the valley who will fight?"

"One," she answered. "Just one, and he won't fight unless he has help. His name is Frank Clemens. He's a teacher and he runs a Sunday school for us, and raises vegetables which we buy. Hearn wanted everyone to believe that the climate in the valley was too severe for anyone to raise a garden, but Frank proved him wrong. Now Hearn raises a big garden on H Ranch."

"Is Clemens married?"

"No."

"Why does he stay?"

"He hates Hearn, too. He says that Hearn's sins will catch up with him, and he wants to be around when they do. You see, he was in love with Jean Phipps." Ellie rose, her tone defiant as she added, "Jean's father is Hearn's foreman, but he hasn't used a gun on Hearn, and he's not old and crippled."

"I'm sorry for what I said about your father." Hugh realized then how much he had hurt her. "Where'll I find Clemens?"

"Probably at home. He lives next to the schoolhouse north of here. You won't have any trouble finding his house. It's the only place with a picket fence around it."

He started toward the door, then stopped. "Ellie, did Hearn pay for our meals and rooms?"

"He never pays for anything."

"How much do I owe you? For my folks, too?"

"Meals are fifty cents apiece. The rooms are one dollar a night."

"Three dollars for our meals and two for the rooms. That right?" She nodded. He laid a five-dollar gold piece on the table as she asked, "What are you going to do after you see Frank?"

"I'm going to H Ranch. Hearn promised me a job."

"Don't do it!" she cried. "You hear me? Don't do it."

He left the dining room, saying nothing more, and he heard her pick up the dishes, banging them angrily. Outside, her father was sweeping off the walk. Hugh stopped and held out his hand. "I'm Hugh Moberly," he said.

"I'm pleased to meet you. I'm Ira Dunn." He gave Hugh a limp grip. "I hope everything was all right?"

"Fine." Hugh dropped his hand, looking at the crepe-like skin of Dunn's face, the deep lines, the faded eyes that touched Hugh's face briefly and turned away. "Your daughter's a good cook," Hugh added, and walking around the corner, turned north. He thought of what Ellie had said, about the strong dying or leaving, and the weak staying. That would explain part, at least, of Hearn's strength. He wondered if Frank Clemens would be all that he hoped.

Chapter 9

Hugh found the schoolhouse first, a small log cabin with a flagpole in front and two small buildings and a long shed for horses in the back. As Hugh walked past, he wondered who paid the teacher, and who had put up the buildings and bought the furniture for the schoolhouse. Vic Hearn? Or the people who lived in the valley?

Frank Clemens was hoeing in the garden behind his house. As Ellie Dunn had said, his place was the only one in town with a picket fence in front. Everything about the place was neat and showed care: the grass, the small flower garden directly in front of the house, the fence, which was painted white. Here was evidence of pride which apparently no one else in town possessed.

Hugh walked around the house, thinking that Clemens would be tall and slender, with glasses perched on a long nose, a precise, bookish man who was allowed to stay in the valley because he was no threat to Vic

Hearn. Hugh went on past the woodshed and barn, and opened a gate which was set firmly in a tight wire fence. Most of the vegetables were barely through the ground, growing in long rows which were absolutely clean of weeds.

Clemens looked up and, seeing Hugh, threw down his hoe and strode toward him, smiling genially. He said, "You're Hugh Moberly, aren't you? I'm Frank Clemens."

They shook hands, Hugh thinking he couldn't have been more wrong about the man. Clemens was short, not over five feet two or three inches, with tremendous shoulders and a fine, well-proportioned head. His big hand, hard with calluses, gave Hugh a strong grip, his gray eyes studying him directly and honestly. He wore no glasses, and his nose, instead of being long, was a fat blob surrounded by freckles.

"I'm Hugh Moberly," Hugh said. "How'd you know my name?"

"News gets around fast in a small place like this," Clemens said. "It's hardly likely there would be two strangers in town at the same time."

"My folks . . ."

"But they've already gone on," Clemens said. "Your father is much older, so you couldn't be him." He laughed. "No, my friend, your identity was no mystery. Come into the house and sit down. I'm glad to get out of the sun. Besides, I never work if I can find an excuse not to."

Clemens opened the gate and closed it behind them. "I raise the only garden in town. This fence is one reason. Rabbits are a pest. You'd never get anything above the ground if you didn't keep them out."

They walked on to the house, Clemens taking two steps to Hugh's one. He was about twenty-five or twenty-six, Hugh judged, with a dogged strength about him that Hugh had not found in the valley outside of Vic Hearn. Hugh instinctively liked Clemens, and felt he could trust him, despite the fact that he had learned by hard experience to be wary of all men until he knew them well. Even then he had been disappointed more than once, but Frank Clemens was cast in a mold different from that of any other man Hugh had ever met. The teacher, he was convinced, had no deceit in him. "I've got some coffee on the stove," Clemens said. "I'll build the fire up —"

"Not for me," Hugh said. "I just had breakfast. Fact is, I overslept. By the time I got downstairs, my folks had gone on to H ranch with Vic Hearn." The kitchen, Hugh saw, was immaculate. Clemens led the way into the living room, which was as neat as the kitchen. The furniture was meager: two rocking chairs, a homemade pine table in the middle of the room, a heating stove, and a bookcase set against one wall, every shelf filled. It, too, was probably homemade. But what amazed Hugh was the fact that the house did not resemble a bachelor's quarters. It seemed to have a woman's touch, with white lace curtains at the windows, a rag rug on the floor, and an embroidered runner on the table with tatting on both ends.

Clemens motioned to one of the rocking chairs. "Sit down." He dropped into the other rocker and, taking a pipe out of his pocket, began to fill it. "I rather expected you to call this morning." He tamped the tobacco down and lighted it. "You're looking for an ally." He pulled on his pipe, filling the room with smoke, then took the pipe out of his mouth and looked at Hugh. "I can tell you one thing. I'm your only prospect."

"How did you know I was looking . . ."

"I told you, news gets around. In the first place, we've heard of you. There are always a few cowhands who drift from one range to another looking for work. Some of them are just grub-line riders. You know how that is.

They talk about anyone who has made a name for himself. Outlaw. Gunfighter. Bronc'buster. Sometimes even a preacher who can outshout everyone else. In your case it was your gun skill. Stories like that always grow with the telling; nevertheless, you did get yourself talked about."

"I guess Hearn had heard some of those stories."

"Perhaps, but I doubt that he'd really believe them. That's one of his weaknesses."

"I don't savvy," Hugh said. "What's this got to do with me calling on you?"

Clemens grinned around his pipestem. "I just wanted you to know that your name was not unknown in this valley. Now then. When you first rode in, Hearn told you to take care of his horses, but you didn't. That's an interesting fact, my friend. Taking care of Hearn's horse was not important. Refusing to carry out his order was. Much as I hate everything about Vic Hearn, I would have obeyed simply because I don't care to pull his wrath down on my head. Not yet." Clemens paused, chewing on his pipestem as if working on a new thought. "Let me ask you something. Did you know at the time how completely Hearn controls this valley?"

"Hearn's Valley," Hugh said. "Hearn

93

Creek. Hearn City. The H Ranch. Sure I knew."

"I thought so," Clemens said, satisfied. "So, for reasons which I don't fully understand, Hearn decided to remove you, but he didn't want the onus put on his shoulders. I mean, there must have been reasons other than the fact that you didn't take care of his horse. Well, he fixed it for Joe Pope to drill you, but that backfired because you and Joe knew each other. I'm puzzled about that. Joe's a tough nut. He's killed three men since he's been in the valley. He wouldn't spare you unless he was afraid of you, which is unlikely, or was obligated to you, which is far more likely."

"Your ears are big, Clemens," Hugh murmured.

"Yes, they are," Clemens agreed. "I make it my business to grow them big. That's how I knew you'd come to me. No matter how good you are, you're smart enough to know you're not good enough to do the job that needs to be done here." Clemens spread his hands. "It seemed to me you'd be likely to cast around for help, and if you cast in Ellie's direction she'd name me."

"How does it happen Hearn lets you stay here?" Hugh asked.

"I'm careful," Clemens answered. "Like I

told you, I don't want to bring his wrath down on my head. I listen more than I talk. Besides, folks like me. I teach their children for practically nothing. I take their boys fishing and hunting. I even teach the girls how to tat and embroider, which their mothers don't have time to do and consider wasted effort anyhow. But the girls like it. I started a Sunday school because we don't have a preacher in the valley, and people like that. So Hearn won't remove me unless he has to, and if he does he'll work it carefully."

"You're doing a hell of a lot more talking than listening today," Hugh said.

"I am," Clemens agreed, "and for one reason. I'm building up to some advice. You may not want to hear it. You may not do what I tell you, but I wouldn't be responsible to God or my own sense of honor unless I gave it to you. I know nothing about your folks or what their relationship to Vic Hearn is. I don't even know why they went to H Ranch with Hearn. At the moment it's none of my business. My advice is to you. Leave the valley and leave it today."

Hugh took the makings from his pocket and rolled a cigarette. "Clemens, you know I won't do it."

"I guess I do." Clemens grinned. "I have one more thing to say. Don't go out to H

Ranch. Live at the hotel. Or stay here with me. I'd like to have you. I live a lonesome life. Sometimes I doubt my own good sense for staying in the valley."

Hugh shook his head. "I've got to go to H Ranch." He struck a match, lighted his cigarette, then got up and walked to the front door and flipped the charred match into the yard. He wheeled to face Clemens. "You're right about me coming here to get an ally. How about it?"

"No. Maybe I'm afraid. You can believe it if you wish. Sometimes I'm not sure myself, because a man can rationalize about anything. But, you see, I keep telling myself that the time is not at hand. It's safer and wiser to let him destroy himself."

"I can't wait," Hugh said, and thought of his mother. He remembered Ellie saying that Hearn was a man women both hated and loved, but he was sure his mother had never hated Hearn. She had only loved him; and, loving him, she would not know him or what was in his mind. He shook his head at Clemens. "No, I can't wait. I don't have time."

"All right," Clemens said. "Any man has a right to make his decisions and his mistakes, but, having made them, he must pay for them."

Clemens was smart, Hugh thought. Too smart, so smart he could reason completely around an issue and successfully evade it. Hugh asked, "Will there ever be a right time?"

"I think so." Clemens took the pipe from his mouth and dropped it into his pocket. "Hearn is strong and cruel and ruthless. And predatory. Throughout history men like him have destroyed themselves. Alexander the Great. Caesar. Napoleon. It makes no difference who you name."

"You overestimate Hearn."

Clemens shook his head. "No. I've lived here six years. I've watched him and I've seen what happens to people, especially women. If you haven't heard about Jean Phipps, you will, if you live long enough. Then there's his law that there will be no cattle in the valley except those belonging to H Ranch. Even the Jersey cows belong to him. He rents them to families that have children. Or take the means of transportation which we have: he owns them. He controls what we eat and what we pay for everything."

Clemens rose and walked to where Hugh stood at the door. He said, "People submit to a man like Hearn because they're afraid. As long as they fear him they stay in line, provided that they only fear him. But if he does something to make them hate him, and if there is a leader who capitalizes on that hate, they'll destroy him. I'm waiting for him to do that something. If he's given enough time, he will."

Clemens scratched the back of his stubby neck. "You know, I think something must have happened to Hearn when he was young that made him hate the world. Now he's bound to make the world pay for it. But there is a universal law which applies to his situation. The world can be made to pay only so long, then it exacts its pound of flesh." He looked at Hugh sharply. "You're still going out there, aren't you?"

"Yes."

"And I'm refusing to give you any help. Well, if you're still alive when you leave H Ranch, come to me. You'll have a place to stay any time you want it."

"Thanks."

Hugh held out his hand, and Clemens gave it his hard grip. Hugh left, thinking that Frank Clemens was indeed a strange man. He had not shown his deepest feelings at any time, but that he had some strong ones about Vic Hearn Hugh did not doubt.

Chapter 10

Hugh ate supper that night with his folks in the dining room of Hearn's big house. He found what he expected, sheer luxury in a wilderness of grass and sagebrush: the cherrywood table with its chairs, each upholstered in a different color; the sideboard with its silver dishes; the sprawling candelabra; the hanging lamp with the old-rose base and crystal drops, long bands of twisted metal running to the ceiling instead of the usual chains.

The table was covered by a damask cloth. In the center was the silver caster with its pepper, salt, vinegar, ketchup, and pepper sauce. The ironstone plates showed a hunting scene with a man on a horse, hounds all around him, and other men on horseback in the distance jumping a fence. The cut-glass goblets glittered in the lamplight, as did the silverware beside the plates.

Luxury, all right, Hugh told himself. Even the wallpaper with its pink nosegays was bright and new. Probably there wasn't another ranch house in eastern Oregon like this one, but there wasn't another spread like H Ranch, either, and certainly not another cowman like Vic Hearn.

Hearn did most of the talking during the meal. He could, as Hugh remembered from his visits to the place on the Deschutes, be very entertaining and charming when he chose. He told fantastic anecdotes about a big buckaroo named Shagnasty Bob who was the strongest man on the range, and about a queer recluse who lived in the pines north of the valley and who, because he had a funny laugh that sounded like a goat's baa, was called Billy Goat Pete. He also told about the literary society that met once a month in the schoolhouse in Hearn City. Everyone in the valley went, he said. They had supper, and spent the evening arguing such questions as "Resolved: That the broom is more important than the dishrag." Or, "Resolved: That a mule is more useful than a wife."

Hugh only half listened, for he was watching Jean Phipps through most of the meal, remembering that Ellie Dunn had said Frank Clemens had once been in love with her, and that she was a woman who had first hated, then loved, Vic Hearn. She had a sinuous figure, and made the most of it when she went to the kitchen for anything. She wore a red dress, cut low at the neck, that clung too tightly at breasts and hips.

Attractive, Hugh told himself, the kind of woman who would arouse a man until he was half out of his mind, if he let her. He remembered Joe Pope saying that he had made a try with her, but that he wasn't big enough. Only Vic Hearn would be big enough for Jean Phipps, and she was exactly the kind of woman Hugh expected to find, fitting him as perfectly as the house did.

Jean said not more than a dozen words during the meal. There was a sullen set to her full-lipped mouth, and now and then, when she looked at Hugh's mother, he felt the hate that burned in her so strongly that it reminded him of the crackling of electricity before a storm struck. She would make trouble, Hugh thought angrily, trouble that his mother did not deserve.

Clara Moberly wore the one decent dress she owned, black satin relieved only by the white lace collar. She carried herself with quiet dignity, ignoring Jean. Suddenly Hugh became aware that she was far more beautiful than the other woman, who was half her age, and he thought Jean knew it.

Sam might as well not have been at the

table. He seemed tired and listless, so completely dominated by Vic Hearn that he was little more than a shadow of a man.

When the meal was finished, Hearn produced a box of cigars, offered them to Hugh and Sam, then took one himself. Hating him as he did, Hugh could not deny the strength and power that were in the man. It was almost as if he could achieve anything he wanted simply by willing it. Hugh was not given to premonitions, but he could not rid himself of the haunting fear that this was the last time he would see his parents together, and that the worst kind of tragedy waited for them.

Presently Hearn rose, saying, "I expect you're tired, Clara."

"It's been a hard day," she said, "but we got a lot done after Hugh got here. Our house is real comfortable."

"I was sure it would be," Hearn said.

Jean stood beside her chair as the others left the table. When they reached the maroon portieres that hung in the archway between the dining room and the parlor, she said, "Mr. Moberly, you forgot something." Both Sam and Hugh turned, then Sam moved on into the other room, for the woman's eyes were clearly on Hugh. He returned to the table, certain he had not forgotten anything. When he reached her, she said, "Get your mother off H Ranch."

"I thought you were going to tell me to leave," he said. "Seems like everybody I've met since I came to the valley told me not to come out here."

She looked at him, making no effort to hide her bitter feelings. She said, "You're a man. You can look out for yourself. Your mother can't. Get her out of here."

"I would if I could," he said. "I didn't want her to come in the first place."

"Then you won't do anything?"

"There's nothing I can do," he said. "Believe me, I would if I could."

He turned and walked out of the room, leaving her staring at his back. The others had left the house. He caught up with them in time to hear Hearn say, "Clara, I'll take you to town as soon as I get caught up with the work. I want you to get enough cloth for several dresses. If Bob Orley doesn't have anything you like, we'll order it. Jean can help you. She's good with a needle."

"We can't afford any dresses just now, Vic," Clara said, "but as soon as Sam's worked a while . . ."

"No waiting," he said brusquely. "I'll pay for the dresses. I suppose you're wearing the best one you've got, and it looks like it's

103

twenty years old." They had reached the little house, and now Hearn turned away, saying, "Good night. Hugh, I want to show you a stallion I bought this spring."

Hugh fell into step with him, leaving his parents standing in front of their doorway. Hugh had not looked at their faces. It was dusk, the light so thin he could not have seen their expressions clearly anyhow, but he knew how they felt, his father particularly. This was the way Hearn would work, cutting Sam Moberly down little by little until nothing was left.

When they reached the road, Hearn said, "You were just coming out to take a look around, weren't you, sonny? I was going to give you a thousand dollars if you rode on. Remember?"

"Am I worth that much to you?"

"That much," Hearn agreed. "To be gone."

"Why?"

"Either you know," Hearn answered, "or you're as big a fool as your father, and I don't believe you are."

"I guess I know, all right," Hugh said. "I'm not going to let you do it. I can't get Ma to leave just yet, so I've got to stay. I'll take the job you offered me. You can't back out of it, Vic."

"No, I won't even try," Hearn said, "but maybe you won't like the kind of work I'll give you."

When they passed the bunkhouse, Oscar Phipps came out and walked beside them. He was as big as Hearn, and nearly the same age, Hugh thought, with a sweeping mustache that was trimmed to look exactly like Hearn's, the only difference being one of color. It was black instead of yellow.

Hugh had met Phipps before supper when the foreman had ridden in off the range with the crew. The fact that he must know, as everyone did in the valley, that his daughter was living with Hearn and that he didn't seem to care one way or the other told Hugh all he needed to know about the man. He was probably a good cowman, but that wasn't enough to keep him here, for Hearn was the kind who demanded loyalty, absolute and complete, so Oscar Phipps would be his man without a single thought of his own.

"Hugh's staying," Hearn said to Phipps. "I promised him a job."

"Why, I guess we can find something for him to do," the foreman said. "Might as well get him started tonight."

They reached the door of the barn. Several lighted lanterns hung from nails driven into posts, and by the smoky light Hugh saw four men standing in the center arena that was surrounded by stalls, the mangers beside a narrow runway that circled the barn next to the wall. Joe Pope. The big buckaroo, Shagnasty Bob, was another. Hugh didn't know the other two.

Hugh had not been warned by word or gesture, but he sensed the danger here without a tangible warning. He could have escaped a minute or two before if he had stayed with his mother and father. Hearn would not have pushed in front of Clara Moberly. He might even have escaped if he had told Hearn he was taking the thousand dollars and leaving in the morning. Now there was nothing to do but go inside with Hearn, Phipps pausing to close the door. Joe Pope stood in the shadows away from the others, his face dark with anger. *He knows what's coming,* Hugh thought, *but he'll stay out of it.*

Shagnasty Bob was grinning like a kid at recess when a bunch of boys will have caught the one they're going to haze. He had the biggest forearms Hugh had ever seen on a man, bigger than most men's legs. His face was covered with red splotches, the skin peeling away from some of them. He was ugly and mean, Hugh knew, and very strong.

Perversely, Phipps took time to introduce them: Whitey Mack, whose eyes were the palest Hugh had ever seen, and Curly Holt, his bald head bright in the lantern light. Hugh glanced at Joe Pope, who failed to meet his gaze. Hearn had paused near the door on the other side of the circle from Pope. It was Phipps' deal, for it had been worked out between them. Hugh was sure of that. He laid a hand on his gun, anger building in him. He was in no mood to take a hoorawing.

"Get your hand off that gun," Hearn called. "You pull it and you're a dead man."

"Not by your pistol," Hugh said. "You wouldn't risk it."

"That's why I hired Joe," Hearn said. "I'll risk him."

"You rode out here to get a job, Moberly," Phipps said. "We aim to show you the kind of work you'll be doing. No reason to draw a gun, now is there?"

Hugh dropped his hand to his side. Shagnasty Bob walked to where Pope stood and returned with a wheelbarrow and a manure fork. "There's your tools," Phipps said. "Clean up the barn. In the morning do the corrals. We've been saving this for you."

For a moment Hugh stood perfectly still, staring at Phipps, who was grinning under his mustache. Shagnasty Bob said, "I always wanted to see a gunslick shoving manure. Maybe he oughta work on his knees."

Whitey Mack snickered. "Yeah, gunslick. Down on your knees in the . . ."

Hugh whirled toward the door and started in a headlong charge at Hearn, but Phipps' boot swept out and tripped him. He sprawled face down into the barn litter. Phipps kicked him in the ribs. Hugh knew then that this was no hoorawing.

Chapter 11

Hugh rolled over and got to his feet. He glimpsed Hearn standing in the edge of the light, his gun in his hand. Joe Pope was on the other side of the barn, motionless. In that brief instant of time, Hugh knew that Pope would not make a move to help him. Hugh's revolver remained in his holster. All he had to do was to go for his gun, then he'd be dead and Joe Pope would be blamed for the killing.

They closed in on him, Phipps and Shagnasty Bob on one side, Whitey Mack and Curly Holt from the other. Hugh got a fist through Phipps' guard to his nose. It squashed like a ripe cherry, blood spurting; then Shagnasty Bob threw a massive shoulder against Hugh's side and bounced him across the center arena toward Whitey Mack.

Wheeling, Mack caught Hugh just as Shagnasty Bob had done. Hugh reeled back across the arena, floundering wildly as he tried to regain his footing in the barn litter, but he was off balance and as helpless as a rubber ball being bounced from one boy to another.

Hugh heard Hearn's great laugh, heard him say, "Keep him going, boys, and he'll be flying like a bird."

Shagnasty Bob was moving in to give him the shoulder again, but Hugh broke his momentum enough to turn and dodge the big man. Hugh couldn't get at Hearn, so Phipps was the next best. The foreman had just drawn a sleeve across his bloody nose and lowered his arm, expecting Hugh to be batted back toward Whitey Mack. Hugh swung again and sledged him on the nose a second time.

Injury now was piled on insult. This blow to his already battered nose must have caused Phipps pain that was nothing less than sheer agony. He staggered back, bellowing like an injured bull. When Hugh hit him the second time, he threw away any chance of getting out of the fracas lightly. Hearn called, "You've had your fun. Finish him."

Mack and Holt came at Hugh from the back just as he started to swing on Shagnasty Bob. The blow was never delivered. Mack caught one arm, Holt the other.

They jammed his hands against the small of his back, twisting and sending pain rocketing up both arms. Shagnasty Bob hammered him on one side of the face with an open palm, then hit him on the other side, powerful blows that made everything in front of Hugh tilt and whirl crazily.

Hugh struck out with his right boot, catching Shagnasty Bob in the crotch. The big hand bent over, made motionless by pain so intense that he was paralyzed by it, sweat breaking out all over his face. Phipps moved in on Hugh blood running down his upper lip into his mouth. He slammed a fist against Hugh's jaw, sending his head bobbing back, then drove a blow to the pit of his stomach that drained the air out of his lungs.

"That's enough!" Joe Pope called.

But it wasn't enough for Phipps. He sledged Hugh on the jaw again, knocking him cold. Hugh went slack in the men's grasp, and when they let go he went down in a rubbery fall. Phipps stepped up and kicked him in the ribs, much harder than the first time.

Pope ran forward, gun in his hand. "That's enough, God damn it! Put your gun up, Hearn! Have you all gone crazy? Are you trying to beat him to death?"

111

"It's a good idea," Hearn holstered his gun. "You're soft, Joe. Too soft. Go get your war sack. You're done!"

"Sure I'm done," Pope said in disgust. "I'm quitting, but I've got a month's wages coming."

"You'll get it," Hearn said. "Fetch Moberly's war sack, too. Curly, saddle his horse. Joe, you're taking Moberly with you, seeing as you're such good friends. Get him out of the valley and keep him out."

"He can't ride," Pope said. "You beat him half to death and then expect him to ride."

"He'll ride," Hearn said. "Just get him out of here."

"What kind of a man are you?" Pope demanded. "I've worked for some ornery bastards, but you take the prize. You put four men on Moberly and beat hell out of him, and then expect him to ride. I ought to shoot your guts out."

Silence for a moment, Hearn staring directly at Pope. Shagnasty Bob sat on a pile of oat sacks, his face gray. Phipps kept dabbing at his nose with a bandanna. Mack and Holt stood motionless on the other side of Hugh, who was still unconscious, watching Hearn as they waited for his next order.

"If you want to leave H Ranch alive,

you'd better put that gun up," Hearn said finally. He dug some gold coins out of his pocket and gave them to Pope. "Your month's not quite up, but I'm giving you your full wages for getting Moberly out of the valley."

"Generous. Just like Santa Claus." Pope motioned toward Hugh. "He'll come back. I know him. He'll come back, and don't you forget it."

"If he does, he's dead," Hearn said. "I've been easy on him too long. If the man's so thickheaded he can't get the idea after this, he don't deserve to stay alive. Go on, now. Get his war sack. Curly, saddle his horse. Fetch Pope's animal, too. Maybe you'd better give him a hand, Whitey."

After the three men left the barn, Phipps walked over to the sacks of grain and sat down beside Shagnasty Bob, the bandanna still held to his nose. He said grudgingly, "He must be made of rawhide, Vic."

Hearn shook his head. "He's just a man, Oscar. Right now he ain't much of a man, either."

Shagnasty Bob said, "Pope's right. Moberly will come back. I say to kill him."

That angered Hearn. "What the hell's the matter with you? Did you ever see a man I couldn't handle?"

"No," Phipps said. "I never did. I never saw a man like Hugh Moberly, neither. He ain't natural. From what you told me, don't seem like a man with good sense would have come out here in the first place."

"Then he ain't got good sense," Hearn snapped. "Go fill a bucket of water, Oscar."

Phipps obeyed. Presently Pope returned with the war sacks, his gaze going immediately to Hearn. Then Phipps came in with the water and sloshed it on Hugh's face. Hugh choked and rolled over; he got up on his knees and fell back.

"He's hurt," Pope said. "He can't ride. You ought to be able to see that, Hearn."

"He'll ride," Hearn said. "I'm getting tired of telling you."

No one spoke until Mack and Holt came in with the horses. Pope tied the war sacks behind the saddles, then looked at Hearn; he saw no hint of mercy on his face. Further argument would be futile, perhaps fatal. He had probably said too much already.

Pope motioned toward Whitey Mack. "Help me get him into the saddle."

They lifted Hugh to his feet, but his knees could not support him, and he sagged in their hands. "Hugh!" Pope said sharply. "Hugh!"

Hugh looked at him as if he didn't see

him, his eyes glazed. Hearn said angrily, "Damn it, get him into that saddle and get him out of here! I've seen all of that son of a bitch I want to see. You too, Pope."

Pope nodded at Mack, and together they lifted Hugh into the saddle. He was conscious enough to grip the horn, but Pope had no idea how long he could retain that grip or even stay on the horse. "Hang on, Hugh," Pope said. "Understand? Hang on."

Pope mounted and, leading Hugh's horse, rode out of the barn and turned north, angling toward the road so they wouldn't pass the little house which still had a light in the window. After they reached the road, Pope asked, "Hugh, can you hear me?"

Hugh said something, an inarticulate grunt that had no meaning for Pope. Joe swore, uncertain how badly Hugh had been hurt. He wasn't thinking of the debt he owed Hugh. He'd paid that. He should be sore about the whole business, losing his job and all. He'd tried to get Hugh to stay away from H Ranch, but Hugh had always been that way, bullheaded once he got something into his head. Now that he thought about it, he knew he wasn't sore about losing his job. He'd had all of Vic Hearn he wanted. He should have quit the day Hugh came to the valley.

Well, there were always jobs for a man with a fast gun. Most of them were more dangerous than this one, but what the hell. You expected danger if you got paid for it. Besides, it was the frosting on the cake. Things had been pretty dull around here lately. He'd stayed on this job longer than most. Time he was moving. If Hugh wasn't too bad off, maybe they could throw in together. Hugh Moberly was a damned good partner.

Half a mile from the ranch Pope dropped back to ride beside Hugh. He asked, "You making out all right?"

"Gotta get off," Hugh muttered.

Pope reined up and helped him. He sprawled on the grass, a hand raised to his head. Pope hunkered beside him and rolled a cigarette, uncertain about what to do next. There was a break in the rim a mile to the north. They could follow it to the top and spend the night up there, and the next day, if they had to. They could camp in a clump of junipers and go on the following day.

Then Pope realized this was crazy thinking. Hugh would never leave the valley now. Pope knew him too well. But if he stayed, he'd stay alone. Joe Pope wanted no fight with Vic Hearn. He was glad to get off H Ranch alive.

Chapter 12

Jean Phipps stood at the table in the dining room until the portieres closed behind Hugh Moberly, biting her lips in a desperate effort to keep her anger under control. She had probably made a mistake talking to Clara Moberly the way she had. Well, she wasn't sorry. She'd worked too hard and too long to get what she wanted to let a woman who called herself Vic Hearn's sister move in and take it away from her.

She began clearing the table and carrying the dishes into the kitchen. She was tired and hot from being over the big range half the afternoon. A good supper, Hearn had said. Well, she'd cooked one, and they'd all stuffed themselves like pigs. Now she had to do the dirty work, standing in the hot kitchen and washing dishes while the sweat ran down her body.

She banged the dishes as she washed them, venting her anger on them, and finally succeeded in breaking one of the ironstone plates. She was instantly shocked into a more rational state. Hearn would raise hell when he found out. He'd fetched those plates up from California when he'd brought his first herd to the valley, carefully packing them in barrels, packing them so well he hadn't lost a single one in all the rough miles of that long trip. He'd used them for special occasions through the twenty years he'd been here, and none had been broken. But now one had been broken, and on the very first day Clara Moberly had come to H Ranch.

Jean held the two sections of the plate in front of her, staring at them, the dirty dishwater running back into the pan. She couldn't afford to have Hearn find out. Feeling as he did right now, it might be all it would take to make him fire her.

She carried them into the pantry and hid them. She'd get rid of them permanently tomorrow, maybe bury them in the back yard when Hearn was out on the range She returned to the dishpan, working slowly and carefully. Hearn probably wouldn't want the plates used again for six months. He'd find out then that one was gone, but she'd worry about that when the time came.

Right now she had Clara Moberly to think about. What did she think she was doing, talking about being Hearn's sister? Hearn didn't think of her as a sister, that was sure. Sooner or later he'd bring her into the big house, and Jean would have to wait on her hand and foot. Cook and wash and iron and work her tail off keeping the house clean while Clara Moberly sat around on her behind reading a book. Well, she wouldn't do it. She had to stop it now, but how?

She finished with the dishes, then brought the tub in from the back porch and dipped water into it from the reservoir at the back of the stove. She cooled it with water from the pump, then stripped off her clothes and took a bath, not caring whether anyone came into the kitchen or not. Right now she didn't care about anything except Clara Moberly.

She dried herself, emptied the tub into the sink and, gathering up her clothes, took the lamp from the kitchen table and went upstairs to her room. It seemed cool after the imprisoned heat of the kitchen. She set the lamp down on the bureau, and stood for a time looking at herself in the mirror. Her skin below her neck was very pale, contrasting sharply with the darker hue of her face. Even this early in the season the sun had begun to tan her so that by fall she would be as bronzed as one of Vic Hearn's buckaroos. But maybe it wouldn't be that way this summer. Sam Moberly was a farmer. He could take care of the garden. She had more than enough to do in the house. She'd tell Hearn.

But it didn't make any difference about the color of her face. It was the paleness of her body that he liked. And her breasts, big and rounded and firm. She cupped each with a hand and stood admiring them. She had nothing to worry about, she told herself. Not from another woman forty years old. She shivered, suddenly cold, and going to the closet, put on her maroon robe and tied the cord. She sat down on the bed, wondering what Hearn was doing and how soon he would come to his room. Would he come to her tonight? Or would he go to his own room and lie in bed and think of Clara Moberly?

For a moment she thought of Frank Clemens, who had once wanted to marry her. She'd been only sixteen. She remembered that she had liked him, a queer man who read a lot and used so many big words that she wasn't sure she always understood him. A strange-looking man, with tremendous shoulders and a big head and almost no neck, giving the impression his head had been pounded down into his hard-muscled shoulders. He had always been kind to her. She remembered that above everything else. He had treated her with gallantry and respect, sometimes even reciting poetry to her. She'd made the mistake once of mentioning that to Hearn, and he'd laughed for an hour.

Actually, she hadn't seen Frank very much, not as much as she'd wanted to. She'd been living with her father on one of Hearn's small, outlying ranches south of the valley, a long way from town, but Frank would hire a rig and come after her. He'd take her to a dance, or to a meeting of the literary society where he always took part in the debates, slashing his opponents to pieces with his rapier-like logic.

She remembered the cold November day when Hearn had dropped in unexpectedly after fall roundup and the drive to the railroad at Winnemucca. He'd had dinner with them, his eyes pinned constantly on her as she waited on the table, or sat across from him. For her father's sake, she'd wanted Hearn to like her, but she had been completely unprepared for the offer he'd made.

Her father came into the kitchen as soon as Hearn had ridden away, more jubilant than she had ever seen him. Hearn had just fired the foreman at H Ranch. He wanted

Oscar Phipps to take the job and he wanted Jean to be his housekeeper.

At first she had thought it would be wonderful. She'd be closer to town, she'd see Frank more often, and she'd have more money than she'd ever had before in her life. But it hadn't worked that way. She had the money, all right, and her father had the job he wanted, but Frank never came to see her, and after a night in this house she hadn't wanted him to.

For a time she had hated Vic Hearn, unable to forget the brutality of the first night. Later, she didn't know exactly when, she discovered she loved him. It was not a thing she could explain to herself.

There were, as her father had once told her, just two kinds of people in the valley: those who hated Vic Hearn and those who loved him. Oscar Phipps, like Shagnasty Bob and the rest of them, would have done anything for him. They learned to think and feel and act as he did. Her father even trimmed his mustache in the same manner Hearn did.

She didn't know anyone who hated Hearn, although her father said some who lived in town had no use for him. That was probably Frank, and maybe that snip of an Ellie Dunn who was jealous of her. And now

122

there would be Hugh Moberly. She had felt it tonight and she was sure Hearn knew it. Well, Hearn would get rid of him, in some way or other.

Vic Hearn had an elemental quality she did not understand, but constantly felt. He was like a wind sweeping the earth clean before it. Or a great river in flood time that could not be dammed. Or an avalanche pouring down the side of a mountain, tearing out anything in its path that man had made. That was what Frank used to say about him.

You feared him, she thought, whether you loved him or hated him. She wondered if that fear was responsible for the loyalty that men like her father and Shagnasty Bob and Whitey Mack and the rest of the crew had for him. Then she decided they didn't know themselves. Neither did she. She had never been sure in her own mind how much her willingness to stay here the last four years had been prompted by fear or by love.

She heard him on the stairs and turned toward the door, thinking he would come to her, as he always did when he had been gone for a time. She waited, her lips parted expectantly, but he didn't come. Then she heard him close the door of his room across the hall.

She began pacing around the room, the anger that had been in her an hour ago flaring up again. She needed him just as he must need her. He knew that. She wouldn't be shoved out by that woman. She'd kill her first. She'd kill Vic Hearn before she'd let Clara Moberly have him.

She yanked her door open, crossed the hall, and went into Hearn's room without knocking. He had taken off his boots and lay on the bed, a cigar tucked into one corner of his mouth. He raised up on one elbow and frowned at her. "You could have knocked," he said.

"You don't knock when you come into my room," she said.

She stood in the middle of the room, her hands on her hips, her robe flaring open between her breasts. He sat up and put his feet on the floor. He said, "There's some difference between you coming into my room and me going into yours."

"What difference?" she challenged.

"You work for me," he said. "I don't work for you."

She swallowed, trying to control her anger, but she couldn't. It burned out the fear she had for him, and made her blurt, "When are you bringing that woman into the house?"

He rose, his lips flattening against his teeth. "Don't talk about her. You understand? You're not fit."

"Not fit?" she screamed, all restraint gone from her. "Not fit, after living with you for four years? You bring that bitch here and then you think I'll —"

He reached her in two long strides. He hit her on the side of the face, a hard blow that knocked her back against the wall. He stood there, big hands fisting and opening at his sides. He said, "If you ever call her that again, I'll break your neck! I don't owe you nothing. Not a goddam thing. You've been paid well from the first day you walked into this house."

She raised a hand to the side of her face where he had struck her. For a moment she could think of nothing except that he had hit her. It was the first time he had ever done so. The blow had made the room spin in front of her but only for a moment; then the dizziness was gone.

"You owe me a lot, Vic," she said. "More than you'll ever know, because you don't know what you took from me. I love you. I don't know why, but I know I'll go right on loving you." She walked to the door and opened it, then looked back. "I won't let her have you. I'll kill you before I do."

She went into her room and shut the door. She had controlled herself when she was with him, but she couldn't now, and the tears came. She fell across the bed, crying as she could not remember crying since she was a little girl. He had never indicated what he intended doing with Clara Moberly, and she had no idea why or how she knew, but she knew.

She heard him open the door, but she didn't move. She wasn't crying now. She was too exhausted. He sat down on the side of the bed and put an arm around her. She had told herself only a moment before that she would have nothing to do with him if he came, but she had never been able to resist him when he wanted her, and she couldn't now.

"Vic," she whispered as she turned to him. "Vic, don't ever let me go."

Chapter 13

Complete consciousness returned slowly to Hugh. He felt pain in a dozen places, particularly in the side where Phipps had kicked him. He sat up when he could think coherently, vaguely aware that Pope had asked something about how he felt. He didn't answer, not sure what the gunman had asked, and not wanting to ask him to repeat the question.

It took some time for Hugh to focus his fuzzy mind on what had happened, but presently he was able to remember that Hearn and Phipps had taken him to the barn where the rest had been waiting. He'd had no chance for his gun. They hadn't given him a fair fight. They'd bounced him around, and then two had held his arms while a third had slugged him. Hugh vaguely remembered that Joe Pope had been in the barn but that he had taken no part in the abuse he'd received. Now Pope was with him.

He puzzled over it for a time, then asked, "How'd we get here?"

"Hearn fired me, then told me to take you and git. Said to keep going on out of the valley and stay out. You'd best get back on your horse as soon as you're able to, and we'll mosey."

"What did he fire you for?"

"Said I was soft. Phipps was kicking you after you were down. I put a stop to it. That made Hearn sore."

So he was in the gunman's debt more than ever. Last night in his room in Hearn City. Now this. He said, "We'll whip the bastard."

"Maybe you will," Pope said, "but I won't. I'm getting out of the valley just like he told me. I figured we'd hole up somewhere till you felt like riding, then we'd go find ourselves a job like we had on the Laramie. We make a good team, Hugh. We could get good wages."

"I'm staying here."

Hugh started to get up but sat down at once, his head whirling the instant he was upright. Pope snorted derisively. "You'll play hell staying here. Hearn will kill you next time certain. Gonna be a long time before you're able to fight. Who's gonna hide you and take care of you till you're able to handle yourself?"

Hugh made no attempt to answer. His mind was slow, dulled by the waves of pain that kept beating at his head in a regular rhythm, but he sensed that Pope was right. Still, it made no difference. He had to destroy Vic Hearn. To do that he must stay in the valley.

"Answer me, damn it!" Pope said irritably.

"I'm staying," Hugh said.

Pope groaned. "Is that all you can say? You're the most bullheaded, chuckle-brained, stubborn jackass I ever seen. You'll be alone. Nobody's gonna fight Hearn but you, and you've got no reason to, now. Your folks will be all right."

"I've got reason," Hugh said. "I'm staying."

Pope swore. He got up and stalked to his horse. He mounted and rode off, then returned. "I must be getting as soft as Hearn says. I don't know why I waste time on a mule-headed, stupid bastard like you who don't know when he's well off."

"Nobody's asking you to waste time," Hugh said.

"Get up," Pope said. "I'll take you to town. If I go off and leave you, they'll find you, and next time they'll beat you to death."

Pope took Hugh by an arm and helped him to his feet, then steadied him until the dizziness passed. "Come on," Pope said. "Somebody in town has got to take care of you. Whoever does it will get plugged by Hearn for doing it, but you wouldn't care."

Hugh walked to his horse, reeling a little. He would have fallen if Pope hadn't steadied him. Somehow he got into the saddle and leaned over the horn, holding to it and wondering how he had managed to get this far from H Ranch. Belatedly he caught what Pope had said about Hearn killing whoever took care of him. He cared, all right, but he still had to stay. He'd go to Frank Clemens. Clemens wasn't afraid of Hearn. He'd said for Hugh to come to his place if he got away from H Ranch alive.

They started toward town, Hugh keeping his grip on the horn, every movement of the horse racking his body with pain. It was the longest and most agonizing night of his life. As it wore on, he had the haunting feeling he had spent hours in the saddle and still was no closer to town than when he'd started. Once he thought he could not stand it. He began to weave in the saddle, and would have fallen if Pope had not reached out and gripped his arm.

"Let's stop," Pope said. "You need a rest."

They reined up and Pope helped Hugh off his horse. Moberly lay on the grass, his head throbbing with waves of pain. He couldn't breathe deeply. Even a light breath brought a stabbing knife into his left side where Phipps had kicked him.

"Better change your mind," Pope said. "We can get out of the valley by riding north. We'll pick up some grub at Billy Goat Pete's place and be in the pines by night. We'll both be safe and we won't get nobody into trouble."

"No," Hugh said.

Pope swore and tramped back and forth in front of Hugh, giving way to his anger. Finally he turned to Hugh, saying harshly, "By God, Hugh, how did you ever live this long?"

"A miracle," Hugh answered.

"It sure is. Now I suppose you want me to stay here and fight with you. For nothing, too. Well, I won't do it. I know when it's time to run."

"Go ahead. Run."

For a long time Pope stood staring down at Hugh, the starshine a thin light; then he said, with grudging respect, "You've got guts even if you don't have good sense." He glanced at the sky. "Be daylight in an hour or so. Let's go some more."

Again it was a fight for Hugh to get his foot into the stirrup, and a greater fight to swing his body into the saddle even with Pope's help. When he finally succeeded, the pain in his side was so bad he thought he was going to faint. He fell forward, the horn punching him in the chest. But he didn't quite lose consciousness. He pushed himself upright, holding hard to the horn as he muttered, "Let's ride."

It was still dark when they reached town, dawn an hour away. They stopped in front of the hotel, Pope not knowing where else to go, and Hugh unable to tell him. Pope helped him down, Hugh groaning with every movement of his tortured body. Almost carrying him, Pope got him across the board walk and into the lobby, then Hugh's rubbery legs gave way completely under him and Pope eased him to the floor.

Pope was nervous, wanting to get out of town before it was daylight and regretting the time it took to get a lamp going and pound the desk bell until Ira Dunn finally appeared, buttoning his pants as he came along the hall to the lobby. He looked at Pope, then at Hugh's motionless body, face down on the floor, and he retreated toward the hall, crying out. "Get him into the street! We don't want him dying in here."

Pope cursed him savagely. "I risked my neck getting him to town. Now you can risk yours."

Pope swung around and would have stomped out if Ellie hadn't run into the lobby, a blue robe over her nightgown, her hair falling down her back to her waist. Seeing Hugh, she called, "Is he dead?"

Pope turned back. "Not quite, but he will be if Hearn finds him. They beat him almost to death."

"Who? Hearn?"

"He wouldn't dirty his hands," Pope said. "It was Phipps, Shagnasty Bob, Whitey Mack, and Curly Holt. Phipps kicked him in the side. Reckon he's got some busted ribs."

"Help us get him into bed," Ellie said. "Then take his horse to Frank Clemens' barn. Frank can get rid of him later."

"No, Ellie," her father begged. "We can't keep him here. You know what will happen to us if Hearn finds him in the hotel."

"That's right, Ellie," Pope said. "Hearn told me to get Hugh out of the valley, but he wouldn't go."

"You see?" Ira Dunn said in a frenzied voice. "You see? He'll get both of us killed."

Ellie looked at her father pityingly. "Pa, you go somewhere so you'll be safe, but I'm going to take care of him." She nodded at Pope. "Help me put him to bed."

Her father hesitated, then said, as if against his better judgment, "I'll help, too."

The three of them carried Hugh's limp body down the hall to Ellie's room and laid him on her bed. She asked, "Hearn won't start looking for him right away, will he?"

"No," Pope answered. "He always figures people are going to do what he tells 'em, but sooner or later you can figure on somebody passing the word to him, and then you'll be in trouble."

Pope started toward the door, leaving Ellie looking down at Hugh's battered face. She asked, "What's hell like, Mr. Pope?"

He stopped and looked back at her, astonished. "Why?"

"I was just thinking it wouldn't be bad enough for Hearn, no matter how bad it is."

"Reckon it won't," Pope agreed. "Nothing could be. Phipps would have kicked Hugh to death in the barn if I hadn't stopped it. Hearn was watching, and having a good time doing it."

"Yes," Ellie murmured. "He'd have a good time watching a thing like that." She was silent, physically sickened by the hatred she felt for Hearn; then she glanced at Pope again. "What are you going to do?"

"I'm leaving the valley. Nothing here to keep me."

"There's Hugh. He'll need help. You can't just ride off and leave him like this."

Pope's face turned red. He licked his lips, then said harshly, "I fight for pay. It's the way I make my living. Have you got money to pay me?"

"No."

"Has your pa? Or Frank Clemens? Or anyone else?"

"No."

"Then there's no job for me in the valley. If I don't start looking, I won't find one."

He wheeled and strode out, his spurs jingling. She stood motionless until the sound died, knowing the one man who could be of help was walking out on her and there was nothing she could do to hold him. She said, "Pull off his boots, Pa. I'll get some salve and liniment."

When she returned, her father had removed Hugh's boots and pants and was unbuttoning his shirt. Between them they were able to lift his shoulders from the bed and take off his shirt. Ellie went to the kitchen again and came back with a towel and pan of water. She washed and dried his face as well as she could, being careful not to start the cuts bleeding again. She rubbed salve on his face and, unbuttoning his undershirt, examined his side.

Hugh was groaning with every breath. Ellie turned to her father. "I think he's got some broken ribs. He ought to have a doctor."

"You want me to ride to Canyon City after one?" he demanded incredulously.

"No, I guess not," she said. "Probably the doctor wouldn't come, and if he did everybody in the valley would know Hugh was here. We can't afford that." She poured liniment into her hand and rubbed Hugh's side gently, then pulled the covers over him and tucked them carefully around his shoulders. "Pa, can a man die of a beating like this?"

"Of course he can," the old man said hotly, "and then what are you going to do with his body? You'll get us both shot, I tell you."

She whirled on him, wanting to say he was a coward, that both of them had been just as bad as the rest of the people in the valley who hated Hearn. But she didn't. The sight of her father's pale face stopped the words before she said them. Telling him he was a coward would not make him anything else.

Besides, Ira Dunn was no worse than Bob

Orley in the store or Daugherty in the livery stable or Dutch Myers in the saloon. Or the farmers and freighters who lived in the valley. Only Frank Clemens was different.

"Pa, go see if Pope took Hugh's horse to Frank's barn like I told him. We can't leave the horse in plain sight after it gets daylight. You'd better wake Frank and have him come here."

Grumbling, Ira Dunn left the hotel. Ellie drew a chair up to the bed and sat listening to Hugh's labored breathing. Would he live, she wondered? And what would he do if he did? She had no way of knowing, but she was convinced he would do something, for that was the kind of man he was.

And Hugh Moberly was a man, she told herself, the toughest fighting man who had ever come to Hearn's Valley. He had to live. He had to. Suddenly, and the thought shocked her, she wondered if she loved him. No, she couldn't, having known him for so short a time. But she had never been in love. She knew nothing about it, or how it made a person feel. She only knew she wanted Hugh Moberly to live, wanted it with an intensity of desire she had never experienced before.

Presently Frank Clemens came in through the back door and stood beside her, looking down at Hugh. Finally he said, "It was bound to be this way. The only surprising thing is that he got here alive, and that a man like Joe Pope had enough conscience to bring him."

"Will he live, Frank?" she asked.

"Sure he'll live. He's a hard man to kill. Besides, he's got a job to do." Clemens paused, frowning thoughtfully, then added, "We'd better take him to my house. If Hearn looks for him, he'll start here."

"We can't move him," Ellie said quickly. "Not now."

Clemens looked at her curiously, then nodded. "All right, we'll move him later. I'd better get started with his horse. I'll take him to Billy Goat Pete's place. Pete's got several roans that look a lot like Hugh's horse."

He walked out, leaving Ellie sitting beside the bed. Presently Hugh began to run a fever, and after that there was little Ellie could do but sit beside him, and pray.

Chapter 14

Hearn stopped at the little house immediately after breakfast the first morning that Clara and Sam Moberly were on H Ranch. Sam had just sat down at the table, and Clara was standing at the stove frying flapjacks. The sun wasn't showing yet, but opalescent dawn light was working into the eastern sky. Sam, glancing at Hearn, sensed that he was in trouble for not being ready to go to work.

Hearn put his arm around Clara's waist and hugged her, asking, "How did you sleep?"

"Fine," she said.

Her red-veined eyes and the tired lines in her face showed she hadn't slept well. Hearn, very pleasant and amiable when he came into the room, became stern. "You're here to take it easy and not worry about anything. Or have you forgotten?"

She smiled faintly. "No, I haven't forgotten."

"Hugh left last night," Hearn said. "He gave me a message for you. You're not to worry about him. He just wasn't ready to settle down."

"He wouldn't do that!" Clara cried. "Just go off and not even tell us good-by."

"Well, he did," Hearn said. "He was afraid to tell you to your face. It was easier just to ride off."

Hearn sat down at the table and canted his chair back against the wall. He took a cigar out of his pocket, smelled it, and then rolled it back and forth between his fingers. Finally he said, "Clara, I understand men like Hugh. I guess they just enjoy drifting. Besides, it's safer to keep on the move, because every time they kill a man there's always some relative or friend after them."

Clara brought a platter of flapjacks to the table. "Can I set a plate for you, Vic?"

He shook his head. "No thanks. I just got up from the table. Clara, did you hear what I said?"

"Yes, I heard." She stood looking at Hearn, deeply troubled. "Vic, you weren't talking about Hugh. It's the other men who ride through here that you understand, but not Hugh."

"I understand him, all right. I didn't tell you the truth about him because I thought he might have changed, but he hasn't. His kind never changes. I did tell Sam." Hearn reached for a match in a vest pocket. "Remember, Sam?"

Sam didn't look up from his plate. "Yeah, he told me, Clara."

"Hugh's a gunfighter," Hearn went on. "The minute he got to town, he put on his gun. He's the kind who don't feel dressed up unless he's wearing it. I'd heard of him and the fights he's been in." Hearn struck the match and lighted his cigar. "Fact is, I had a man working for me named Joe Pope who was with Hugh in a range war on the Laramie. I figure they rode out together."

Clara sat down at the table, looking at Hearn and shaking her head. "I can't believe it, Vic. We never raised Hugh to be like that."

"It's not a proposition of how you raised him," Hearn said. "It's what was in him to start with. That's why he couldn't stay home. It's why he didn't take the job I offered him. Thirty a month and found is nothing to a man who can hire out his gun."

Clara rose and filled Sam's coffee cup. Then she sat down again, and Sam, glancing at her, saw she was close to crying. He said gently, "Don't take on about it. Hugh can look out for himself."

"But he could have said good-by," Clara cried. "He could have done that."

"Every man is brave some ways and a coward in others," Hearn said. "Hugh can face a man with a gun in his hand, but he couldn't face his mother and tell her he was going to disappoint her again." Hearn rose, his cigar tucked into a corner of his mouth. "I'm sorry, Clara. I'll do anything I can to make you happy, but talking Hugh into staying was something I couldn't do. I tried. I talked myself black in the face, but I couldn't change him."

"I'm not blaming you, Vic," she said miserably. "I know you tried."

"I don't need any more riders just now," Hearn said, "but I would have given him a job on your account. Anyhow, I don't want you to get upset about him. In a month or two you'll probably get a letter from him. Hard to tell where he'll be. Arizona. Montana. Colorado. But wherever he is, he'll be all right."

"Yes, Vic," she said. "I'm sure he will."

Hearn walked to the door. "I've got some riding to do. I expect to be gone several days. Sam, I'll show you what to do while I'm gone."

Hearn went out, and Sam took his hat off a nail in the wall and followed him, leaving

Clara at the table. Sam had to trot to keep up with Hearn's long strides as he walked toward the barn. He was like a docile dog, Sam told himself bitterly, taking Hearn's orders with no power whatever to make any decisions for himself.

Because of Clara, he had given up the right to call himself a free man. Suddenly, and it was the first time he had admitted it to himself, he realized the magnitude of the mistake he had made, and he wished, with a deep, wild yearning, that he had ridden away with Hugh.

"I'd better make something clear," Hearn said. "I thought you'd figure it out for yourself, but I see you haven't. I'm paying you one hundred dollars a month. That's a hell of a lot of money, Sam."

Hearn paused, turning his head to look at Sam. *He wants me to tell him he's generous,* Sam thought. *He wants me to get down in the dirt in front of him, but I won't do it.*

"If you hadn't been lazier'n hell, you'd have made a good living where you were." Hearn changed directions so they were headed for the long shed north of the barn. "That was all right when you had your own place, but you're working for me now, and you're going to earn your wages."

Still Sam said nothing. He couldn't look

at Hearn. He stared at the ground, breathing hard, certain that Hearn would never talk to him this way in front of Clara. He wondered if Hearn had talked the same way to Hugh last night. If he had, Hugh had plenty of reason to leave.

They reached the shed, Hearn pointing to the row of mowing machines and rakes. "This is where you'll start. We usually begin haying right after the Fourth. I want you to see that every machine is in good shape. Sharpen the sickles. Replace any blades that need it." He pointed to the bench at the end of the shed. "You'll find rivets and extra blades in the box yonder. There's an oil can and a grindstone."

"All right, Vic," Sam said heavily.

Hearn grinned, shoving his hands under his waistband. "The harness needs some fixing. See that you get it done. In between times, you can work in the garden. Jean usually does it, but now that you're here the job's yours. Jean will tell you what to do. You'll probably have to get water on the garden in a day or two. There's a ditch that comes out of the creek a couple of miles upstream. It hasn't been cleaned out since last summer."

Sam lifted his gaze to Hearn's face and looked away. "In between times," Hearn had said. But there wouldn't be any "in be-tween times." Sam asked in a low tone, "What are you trying to do, Vic?"

Hearn laughed and slapped him on the back. "I'm trying to get my money's worth out of a bad investment." He walked away, still laughing.

Sam stared at his back. Hearn had never mentioned the beating he'd taken the day before Sam and Clara were married, but it was plain that he hadn't forgotten. He'd waited all this time to get square for that beating, and now, after more than twenty years, he had his chance.

Sam watched the crew rope horses and saddle up. He recognized Shagnasty Bob from Hearn's description the night before, a mountain of a man who looked strong enough to do the fantastic things Hearn had told about. Oscar Phipps, the foreman, was with them, his nose swollen and discolored. Apparently it had been broken, for it gave the odd appearance of pointing one way while he went in another.

The men mounted, some of the horses bucking until the kinks were worked out of them; after considerable laughing and shouting and good-natured banter, they headed south, Hearn in the lead, riding like a king at the head of his band of retainers, arrogant and proud and all-powerful. As far as the valley was concerned, Sam thought bitterly, he was king, maybe even with the power of life and death over his people.

Sam worked all morning on the mowing machines, spending most of the time sharpening sickles, the grindstone making a steady scream in the morning air. At noon he walked toward the house, so tired he didn't know how he could get through the afternoon. When he'd been home, he had always taken a nap after dinner, but he couldn't do that now.

Jean Phipps came out of the big house, calling, "Moberly!"

He stopped, not wanting to spend the energy it would take to walk to her. He asked, "What is it?"

"Come here!" she said, her voice holding the same arrogance of tone that Hearn had used.

He walked to her, thinking it was easier to do that than stand here arguing. She placed her hands on her hips, looking at him as if he were a servant. That was just about the size of it, he thought sourly.

"The garden needs hoeing, Moberly," Jean said. "You tend to that this afternoon."

"I've got to work on the mowing machines," he said.

"Vic won't need them for a month," she said. "The garden's got to be saved now. If it don't rain in a couple of days, you've got to get water on it. In the morning you'd better start cleaning out the ditch."

"But Vic said —"

"He's gone," she said tartly, "and while he's gone you'll take orders from me. If you don't like it, you can leave."

She whirled, her skirt rippling outward and showing her trim ankles. She walked to the big house, her round hips swaying with what would have been a titillating rhythm to a younger and less tired man. Sam turned and went into the little house.

Clara heard him from the kitchen, and called, "I'll have dinner on the table right away so you can get back to work."

He dropped into a rocking chair. For the first time in many years he was thoroughly angry with her. He shouted, "By God, I don't want to go back to work!"

She ran into the living room, shocked by what he had said and the tone he had used. She asked, "What's wrong, Sam?"

"Everything," he said. "I'm not going to work for a bastard like Vic Hearn. I'm not going to stay. I'm going back to the Deschutes."

"Then you'll go alone," she said angrily.

"You're ungrateful. After what Vic's done for us, and you sit there and call him a name like that."

She stomped back into the kitchen and began rattling pans. He said, "I'm sorry, Clara." He stopped. No, he wasn't sorry. Not for the name he had called Hearn; he was sorry because he had made her angry. He got up, walked into the kitchen, and sat down at the table. "Don't get mad, Clara. I'm so tired I don't know what to do."

She came to him, made contrite by his apology, and put a hand on his shoulder. "Of course you're tired. I've got a good dinner for you. After you eat, you lie down and take a rest. You'll feel better then."

"The Phipps woman wants me to work in the garden this afternoon," he said, "but if I don't get the mowing machines in working order by the time Vic gets back, he'll be sore."

"No, he won't. He doesn't expect you to do more than you can."

She returned to the stove. "I don't know why he can't get rid of that woman, I could keep house for him better than she can. He might as well save her wages. We could live over there just as well as here."

Sam leaned forward and put his head on his hands. He saw Vic Hearn in a different light than he ever had before. Now he could only blame himself for not knowing what the man was a long time ago, but that was the wisdom of hindsight. Clara didn't even have that. She would never see Hearn for what he actually was unless he did something or said something in front of her as he had to Sam this morning.

But he won't, Sam thought miserably. *He never will.*

Chapter 15

Hugh was slow to shake the fever, slow to remember exactly what had happened, and even slower to regain his strength. For days everything that took place in his room was hazy, all sight and sound distorted and out of proportion.

He slept much of the time. Quite often he would wake up suddenly, gripped by a terrible paroxysm of fear, crying out in words that ran together and were unintelligible. He could not relax unless Ellie was there beside him, holding his hand and rubbing his forehead, and talking softly to him; then he would drop back onto the pillow, sweat breaking through the skin of his face.

Once Frank Clemens was there when Hugh had a nightmare. After Ellie had quieted him, Clemens followed her into the kitchen. He asked, "Can you tell what it is that bothers him?"

"He's afraid," she said, "but not for himself. I can't make much sense out of what he says, but I think he's worried about his mother."

Clemens nodded. "Ellie, one of these days somebody will be in the hotel when he's hollering that way and hear him. Maybe Hearn or some of his men. What will you do then?"

"I don't know," she said. "Maybe the good Lord won't let it happen."

"Don't talk that way, Ellie," Clemens said sternly. "The good Lord doesn't have any hands. Just ours."

After the fever was gone, Hugh lay there listlessly, his cheeks gaunt, his eyes too large for his face. He recalled some of the vague impressions he'd had and was not really sure any of them had happened: of Ellie slipping in and out of the room, but always there when he needed her; or old Ira Dunn sitting beside his bed or holding a cup of water to his cracked lips; of Frank Clemens in the chair beside the bed. On several occasions Clemens brought his shaving gear and shaved him, and after that he would drop off to sleep again. But never anyone except those three. Gradually Hugh realized how it was. One night when Clemens was sitting with him, Hugh said, "No one knows I'm here except you and Ellie and her pa. That right?"

"That's it," Clemens said. "We're hoping no one finds out till you're on your feet. As soon as you're able to walk, I'm taking you to my place. You'll be safer there."

"So will Ellie," Hugh said.

"That's right" Clemens agreed. "You owe your life to Ellie. And to Joe Pope for bringing you here."

"Where is Joe?"

"I don't know. Hundreds of miles from here by now, I guess."

Hugh thought about that for a minute, knowing that Pope could take care of himself. But Ellie was another problem. He had never owed anyone else the debt he owed Ellie, and the knowledge of it made him uncomfortable. The fear of what would happen to Ellie if Hearn found him here made him more uncomfortable. "Better take me to your place now," Hugh said. "I sure don't want to get Ellie into trouble."

"Ellie won't hear of it yet," Clemens said, "but I think by the first of next week you can be moved. It's your side that worries us. Those ribs won't heal unless you're absolutely quiet."

"Where are my clothes?"

Clemens grinned. "Ellie washed them. I don't know where she put them. She won't take any chances on you putting them on and walking out of here before she's ready to let you go."

Ellie came in with a bowl of chicken broth. Clemens rose and let her have the chair. She had been spooning it into Hugh's mouth, but now he said, his tone irritable, "Put another pillow under my head. I can feed myself."

"He's cranky," Clemens said. "That's a good sign, Ellie."

She smiled. "I guess it is. All right, Frank, lift his head and I'll slip this other pillow under it."

For the first time, the broth had a good taste to it. When the bowl was empty, Hugh said to Ellie, "Frank says you've hidden my clothes. I guess there's no use arguing with you about fetching them, but I want my gun."

Ellie glanced at Clemens, who nodded. "I think he should have it. He'd be plain helpless without it if Hearn found him."

"He won't find him," Ellie said passionately. "I'll kill him before I'll let him. . . ."

"Sure," Hugh said. "You'll kill him. Or I will. Or Frank will, but this isn't the time."

"Oh, you talk just like Frank," Ellie said rebelliously. "Why do we have to wait? And how long? Hasn't Vic Hearn done enough. . . ."

"Yes," Clemens agreed. "He's done more than enough. I don't know how long we'll have to wait, but I can tell you why we're waiting. When the time is right, Hearn will destroy himself. We need patience. If we push it now, we'll be responsible for the unnecessary death of a lot of people."

This wasn't Hugh's reasoning. He thought of his folks on H Ranch, but he had no way of knowing how much time he had. There seemed to be no reason to think either was in any immediate danger. Hearn would treat Hugh's mother well, and his father wasn't likely to be in any danger as long as there was summer work to be done on H Ranch. Besides, Hearn would draw suspicion upon himself if an accident happened to Sam Moberly.

There was only one reason to wait. His body had to have time to heal. Judging by the way his side felt, it would be quite a while. Another factor entered into his thinking. Hearn had to be handled in such a way that Hugh's mother would never know the full truth. She would be happier if she could always think of Hearn as the kindly man she believed him to be.

Ellie had been glaring at Clemens. Now she said, "Patience! I'm clean out of it, Frank."

"Get my gun," Hugh said wearily. "I don't want to be caught like a sitting duck."

She turned her gaze from Clemens to Hugh, then left the room without another word. When she returned a moment later, she had Hugh's gun. He checked it, saw that an empty was under the hammer and that the cylinder held five loads. Then he slipped the revolver under the pillow.

"Ellie," Hugh said, "I can't repay you for what you've done for me, but —"

"Hugh Moberly," she broke in, "don't ever talk to me about repaying me. There's nothing I can do if I took the rest of my life to repay you for what you did the first night you were here."

She stalked out, her heels hammering on the floor. Clemens asked, "What was that?"

Hugh told him, then added, "You can talk about patience, Frank, but it's not for me. Or Ellie."

"Then patience is not the right word," Clemens said. "I can't risk failure, Hugh. That's all. This is not a thing to gamble on. I can tell you that if we pick the wrong time, we'll fail."

Hugh understood, and nodded agreement. After Clemens left, he got up and walked across the room and back, then fell into bed, so weak that he hurt. His side started to throb again, and although he realized he might tear the muscles or destroy the knitting of the bones that had taken place, if his ribs actually had been broken, he knew he had to exercise or he'd be all summer regaining his strength. Every day for the rest of the week he walked the length of the room and back, staying on his feet a little longer each time. By Saturday he was able to stay up for five minutes or more without feeling that he was falling apart, as he had the first time. Late that Saturday Vic Hearn came to town with his crew.

When Ellie saw Hearn and his men dismount in front of Dutch Myers' saloon, she ran into Hugh's room and told him, then added, "I'm going to lock the door. Hearn has no reason to believe you're here, but I don't think we ought to take any chances." She closed and locked the door, and dropped the key into her apron pocket. Then she ran across the kitchen into the pantry, and took a gun off a shelf where she had hidden it. It was a small revolver which had belonged to her father, but she knew he would never use it, so she had stolen it from his room.

If her father had missed it, he had said nothing about it. Perhaps he was glad to be rid of it, but Ellie never doubted her ability to use it if the time came. She had told herself repeatedly that Vic Hearn would never come into her bedroom again.

She was busy at the range when her father came into the kitchen. "They're here," Ira Dunn said. "The whole kit and kaboodle of 'em. We'll have 'em all for supper in another half-hour."

"We've got enough to feed them," she said. "Don't you worry, Pa. You peel these potatoes. I'll fry them."

The men came in presently, filling every table in the dining room, most of them liquored up enough to be noisy. Ellie took their orders, ignoring Hearn's appreciative gaze. He sat at a table with Oscar Phipps, Shagnasty Bob, and Whitey Mack.

It was the first time Ellie had seen Phipps since the night Hugh had been beaten. He'd told her how he'd hammered the foreman's nose, but she wasn't quite prepared for the comical way his nose, still badly bruised and swollen, pointed to one side above his great mustache. She hurried back into the kitchen, wanting to giggle and knowing she must not. She couldn't get hysterical, either, she told herself. She was going to need her presence of mind for the next hour or two.

She got the men fed, with her father helping in the kitchen. They straggled out, anxious to return to their drinking, and Ira had to stay at the desk to take their money. Hearn remained at his table, smoking a cigar, his eyes following every move Ellie made. The gun in her apron pocket seemed as heavy as a .45, and she wondered if Hearn noticed the sag on that side of her apron.

He rose, the cigar half smoked. "A good meal, Ellie. I guess you're about as good a cook as Jean."

That made her angry. "I'm a better cook," she said, and carried a load of dirty dishes into the kitchen, the sound of Hearn's laughter following her.

When she returned to the dining room, Hearn was in the lobby. She heard him toss a coin on the desk, probably a dollar, judging by the way it rang. He said, "Keep the change, Ira."

"Thank you kindly, Mr. Hearn," her father said in the servile tone he used with him.

"No thanks necessary," Hearn said. "It was a good meal, and I'm glad to get a change of grub once in a while. The boys are, too." There was a pause, then he asked, "You seen Joe Pope lately, Ira?"

"No," her father said. "Not for a long time. Ain't he working for you no more?"

"Not by a damned sight," Hearn said. "He packed up and left. Been a couple of weeks or more. I figured he might have stopped here on his way out of the valley."

"Seems like he did, now that you mention it," Ira said reluctantly. "Said you'd beaten young Moberly up."

Ellie stood motionless beside one of the tables, her heart hammering crazily. She felt like shaking her father. If he only knew enough to keep his mouth shut. Now Hearn would start asking questions.

"Oh, I didn't beat him up," Hearn said. "It was Oscar. You see his nose? Moberly fixed it so it won't never look right again. Oscar will kill him if he ever finds him."

"Maybe he won't find him," Ira said.

"I'm curious," Hearn went on, "about why Pope stopped here. Did he have Moberly with him?"

"No," Ira said.

"I figure you're lying, Ira," Hearn said amiably. "Might be you even kept him for a spell. Maybe he's still here."

"No, he ain't!" Ira shouted. "He ain't here."

Ellie slipped into the lobby and stood beside the desk. She said, "Mr. Hearn, will

159

you please go away and leave us alone?"

He turned to her, his mouth pursed out around the cigar stub. "I got a notion you're sitting on the anxious seat, Ellie," he said. "Now I'm wondering why. I think I'll take a look in your rooms just to satisfy my curiosity."

He glanced at Ira, who stood behind the desk, stiff and plainly frightened, then he turned toward the stairs. Ellie's first reaction was one of panic. She couldn't stop Hearn. No one could stop him. He was a man who couldn't be stopped. Sooner or later he would find Hugh, and Hugh was too weak to fight.

But she had to try. She darted across the room and reached the stairs before he did. She cried passionately, "You don't have any right to search our rooms! You turned the hotel over to us. It's our home. It's the only one we've got."

Hearn laughed softly. "That's right. And don't forget that if I took this one away from you, you wouldn't have any."

"I haven't forgotten," she said bitterly, "but we'd be better off without any home than having you paw through everything we own."

"You're like all women," he said, plainly pleased by her resistance. "You pretend you're fighting me, but every minute you're alive you're afraid I'll let you alone."

He put his arms around her and drew her toward him. His face was very close to hers, the hairs of his mustache almost touching her face. She sensed the animal hunger that was gnawing at him. Suddenly she was frightened for herself as well as for Hugh, and this time he could not help her as he had before.

She placed her hands against his chest and tried to push him away, but it was as futile as pushing at a mountain. Suddenly she was afraid she was going to faint, for the terrifying thought ran through her mind that if he once possessed her she would belong to him just as Jean Phipps did, that he would start a fire burning in her that would make her desire him as he desired her. If that happened, she would be destroyed as so many others had been, as Jean Phipps would be in time.

He moved his hands to touch her breasts, then let them slide along her body to her hips. She remembered the gun in her apron pocket. When he released her, she made a frantic effort to lift the gun from her pocket; but she had barely freed it when he grabbed her wrist, twisted the gun from her fingers and tossed it the length of the lobby.

"By God, you're a fighter!" he said, laughing. "I like that. You're too smart to give in quick and easy."

Ira was still behind the desk, watching, but he couldn't stand it any longer. He cursed Hearn and came at him, his fists swinging. Hearn hit him once, knocking him halfway across the lobby. He said angrily, "Behave yourself, old man." Then he looked at Ellie. The smile was gone from his lips; his breathing made a steady, rasping sound. He said, "You play the game good, Ellie. Real good, but don't play it too long. I never saw a horse I couldn't break. Don't forget there's a lot of ways to break a horse, and some of them are pretty hard on the horse."

He turned and started up the stairs. "Go ahead and look!" Ellie screamed at him. "Look under the beds. Look in the closets. You won't find Hugh Moberly up there."

He went on, not looking back at her. She glanced at her father, who was on his knees, feeling his jaw. He was all right, she saw. She ran along the hall, knowing she had only a minute or two in which to get Hugh out of the hotel. She unlocked his door, wishing she had taken time to pick up her gun. She knew she must never let him get close to her again. She would kill him first.

She opened the door. Hugh was sitting on the edge of the bed, his gun in his hand. He was very close to death, she knew, within the two or three minutes it would take Hearn to search the upstairs rooms and come back down to the lobby. He was certain to come here next. In that moment she became acutely aware of her love for Hugh, and realized that he was the first man who had ever walked into her life that would never leave it.

"You've got to get out of here," she said, trying to keep the terror she felt from creeping into her voice. "You'll have to go to Frank's house."

He shook his head stubbornly. "I'm not going off and leave you with him. I'll shoot him the minute he pokes his head through that door."

"Oh, Hugh," she cried in exasperation, and knew there was only one way to persuade him. "You'll bring his whole bunch on top of us. You'll get us all killed."

"I can't leave you alone. . . ."

"I'll be all right." Only seconds now, she thought. "You have a right to get yourself killed, but you don't have a right to bring your troubles down on our heads and get us killed, too."

He could not stand against that argument. He got up and crossed the room. "My clothes . . ."

"You haven't got time. Come on!"

She put an arm around him, not at all sure he could walk to Frank Clemens' house, but he'd be safer flat on his face out there in the darkness than he would be in her room. She stayed with him until he was out of the hotel and across the back yard.

"I've got to go back," she said. "I can't let him think I left to warn you. You've been in Frank's house. You'll find it. Just keep going."

She whirled and ran back into the hotel. Hearn was still upstairs. She went into her room, glancing around to see if there was anything there that would hint at the fact that Hugh had occupied the room. Just the bottle of liniment on the bureau. She dropped it into a drawer and closed it, then straightened up the bed.

She could not forget what Hearn had told her, that he hadn't seen a horse he couldn't break. Women and horses confronted him with the same challenge. If she stayed, and if Vic Hearn lived, he would eventually break her. It was as inevitable as the sunrise, for she knew the strength of the man.

Chapter 16

Hugh stood leaning against the wall of a shed after Ellie left him, his eyes on the back of the hotel. She was right. He could have shot Hearn, but he couldn't have fought Hearn's crew. They'd rip the hotel apart, maybe burn it, and Ellie and her father would be killed.

When Hugh thought about what had happened to him in the barn at H Ranch, he knew there was nothing that men like that would not do. No, he couldn't bring his troubles down on Ellie and her father. They had risked too much for him already.

He went on toward Clemens' house, walking slowly, his knees threatening to give with every step. He was wearing nothing except a nightshirt Ellie had given him. One of Clemens', probably. It was too big in the shoulders and far too short. His bare feet hurt with every step. Rocks bruised them. He picked up briars. A piece of glass cut his right heel. Twice he had to sit down, his legs refusing to carry him. He was panting as if he had just come in from a hard run, and sweat was pouring down his body. He cursed his weakness, his inadequacy in the face of the job that he had to do.

He should have insisted on going to Clemens' house sooner, or asked Clemens to stay in the hotel with him. Hell, there were a dozen things he should have done, but it was too late for any of them. Now he could only hope that Ellie would not suffer because she had given him a refuge. He had heard nothing about his folks since they had gone to H Ranch and he'd taken the beating. They were all right, he told himself. He would have heard if they weren't. Hearn certainly would not harm his mother, and he wouldn't do anything to Hugh's father as long as the summer work had not been done. So Hugh had until late summer or fall, and Hearn would be taken care of long before that.

He had no idea of time, but it seemed to him he had been hours going the short distance from the hotel to Clemens' house. He was in the front of the schoolhouse when he fainted. He didn't know it was coming. He started to fall, when he came to he was on his face in the dirt. For a moment he couldn't remember what had happened.

His first thought was for his gun. He began feeling around in the dust, wildly, crazily, wondering in panic if he had dropped it somewhere between here and the hotel. Then his searching fingers found it, and he sat up, gripping the walnut butt of the gun, the thought coming to him that it was the most important possession he had, the only tool which could change life in Hearn's Valley.

He got to his feet again, so dizzy that the whole world seemed to be whirling and plunging in front of him. He reached the corner of Clemens' picket fence and held to it for support. After he had rested a full minute, he moved slowly along the fence until he reached the gate, then started up the path toward the house. He was almost to the porch when his legs gave under him again, but this time he did not lose consciousness. "Frank." He tried to shout the word, but it was far from a shout. He tried again, "Frank," and this time Clemens heard him. The door was flung open, the lamplight falling across the front yard past Hugh. He said, "Help me inside, Frank. I'm beat."

"My God, Hugh, what happened?" Clemens lifted him to his feet.

Hugh said, "Hearn was looking for me.

Ellie wanted me to get out of the hotel."

With Clemens' strong arm around him, he crossed the porch and went into the house. Clemens eased him down at full length on the couch. He said, "I'll get a drink," and disappeared into the kitchen. Hugh shut his eyes, resenting his weakness and wondering if he would ever be any good again. Clemens returned with a tumbler half full of whisky. Hugh sat up long enough to drink it, then sank back.

"I felt pretty good in bed," he said. "I kept exercising a little, walking across the room and back, but I didn't know I was this bad off. I'm not strong enough to skim the cream off a pan of milk."

"You will be," Clemens said. "Time's the only answer. Trouble is, you're an impatient man."

"Could you be patient if you was me?"

"I don't know," Clemens said. "Anyhow, it's an academic question. I'm not you."

"Go over to the hotel, will you, Frank? Take a gun. I don't remember that I've ever been really scared before, but I'm sure scared for Ellie. I didn't want to leave her, but she said she'd be safer with me gone."

"She wasn't thinking about herself, Hugh," Clemens said. "She never does. She knew you'd be safer."

Hugh shut his eyes, sick with the knowledge that he had gone off and left her at a time when she needed help. "I should have stayed," he said bitterly. "Damn it, I should have stayed."

"No, you did right," Clemens said. "It was the only thing you could have done. Ellie can take care of herself, but I'll go over and see, just to make you feel easier."

"Take a gun," Hugh said.

Clemens nodded, and stepped into the bedroom. When he returned, he had a .45 stuck under his waistband. "I'll be right back."

Hugh didn't move during the time Clemens was gone. He wasn't panting now and the sweat had dried on him, but he was thoroughly exhausted. It was an effort even to breathe.

Ellie was with Clemens when he returned. She knelt beside the couch, her hand feeling Hugh's forehead. "I'm sorry, Hugh. I knew what I was doing to you, but I thought it would be worse if he found you in the hotel."

"I'm ashamed," he said. "I thought you were worried about yourself, but I should have known better."

"Maybe I was."

"No, it was me." He reached out and

169

touched her hair. "Ellie, I've never known a girl like you before. I wish I could find the right words. . . ."

"Don't try, Hugh," she said softly. "I'm not very proud of myself. Or of Pa, either. I guess Frank is the only one in the valley who has any right to be proud."

"Me?" Clemens laughed shortly. "Not me, Ellie. Maybe someday I'll do something I can be proud of, but I haven't done it yet."

"Get me some warm water and a towel, Frank," Ellie said. "He's cut his feet badly."

Hugh lay motionless, his right hand hanging down beside the couch, his gun on the floor. He watched her, wondering where she got her tough core of courage. Not from Ira, who was as near nothing as any man Hugh had ever met. But again, as Ellie had said more than once, her father was no different from Myers or Bob Orley or Daugherty or any of the rest who lived in the valley. Maybe obedience to Hearn had become a habit. Maybe it wasn't entirely fear, as Hugh had supposed.

Finished, Ellie rose and handed the pan of water and the towel to Clemens. "You've got a bad cut, Hugh. I'll be back tomorrow and look at it again." Clemens went into the kitchen with the pan and towel.

Hugh asked, "What happened after I left?"

"Nothing much. Hearn banged around the way he does. He looked into Pa's room and in mine where you were. He finally remembered he had a big game waiting for him in the saloon, so he left the hotel."

"What was Ira doing all that time?"

It always made her angry when he inferred that her father was short on courage, and it did now. She said sharply, "All men aren't like you. You keep forgetting that. You won't believe it, but Pa tried. Hearn had his hands on me, and Pa tackled him. Hearn hit him and knocked him down."

Hugh sat up, bracing himself with both hands against the couch at his sides. "Hearn didn't . . . do anything to you?"

"No," she said impatiently. "This was before he went upstairs. I was trying to keep him from searching the rooms."

Suddenly Hugh's hatred for Hearn exploded in him. All he knew was that he had to kill the man, that no woman was safe from him as long as he was alive. Hugh's mother on H Ranch. Ellie here in town.

He picked his gun up off the floor. "I'll kill him. I won't let him leave town alive."

He got to his feet just as Clemens came back into the room. He dimly heard Ellie say, "Hugh, why do you have to keep trying? You're too sick . . ." That was all he remembered, for he was falling again and the floor rushed up to meet him.

When he came to, he was in Clemens' bed and Ellie was gone. Clemens sat beside him, smoking his pipe. When Clemens saw that Hugh was conscious, he said, "You're the damnedest man I ever was around. Have you lost all your sense?" He shrugged. "I guess you can't help being what you are, but try to look at this rationally. You can't whip Hearn in the shape you are now, so quit trying."

"Ellie?"

"She went back to the hotel. She's all right."

"Maybe I have lost all my sense," Hugh said bitterly, "but the main thing is I'm ashamed of myself for not killing the bastard when I had a chance."

Clemens pulled steadily on his pipe. "I know, but it's worse with me. I've had a dozen chances, but I've never taken any of them. If you'd been here and I'd had your help, I think I would have tried, but I'm not sure, Hugh. Sometimes when I get to thinking about him . . ."

He stopped. Hugh, looking at him, understood how it was. Frank Clemens was not a killer. He was no part of a gunman, and he knew that if he ever faced Hearn he would be committing suicide. But he could not bring himself to shoot Hearn in the back. "He's like a sheep-killing dog that's got a taste of blood," Hugh said. "He can't stop. No man who fights him is safe, and no woman is safe with him, either. My mother out there, Frank. And Ellie here."

"I know, I know." Clemens rose and looked down at Hugh. "He's a spoiler of women. He doesn't give a damn for Ellie, but she's a woman he hasn't had and he won't be happy till he's successful. He's a pestilence. He's sick, in his own way. I've thought of it, Hugh. Believe me, I've thought of it until I'm half crazy. If I get crazy enough, I suppose I'll take a shotgun and blow his head off. I keep telling myself, as I told you at first, that someday he'll destroy himself, but now I'm afraid we can't wait that long."

"I won't," Hugh said sharply.

"No, I'm sure you won't," Clemens said. "Now, in spite of all my efforts to be logical, I'm afraid I won't wait, either. Well, you'd better try to sleep. As soon as you're able to ride, I'll take you to Billy Goat Pete's place. It's out of the way and you'll be safe there. Pete's one man we can trust."

Clemens blew out the lamp and left the room. Staring after him, Hugh was sorry for him. Frank Clemens was having trouble living with himself, and he would go on having trouble as long as Vic Hearn was alive.

Chapter 17

June was a dry month, and the hottest anyone in Hearn's Valley could remember. Because of the drought, the garden on H Ranch made incessant demands on Sam Moberly. He spent days cleaning the ditch, and by the time he had water on the garden the weeds were ahead of him. The result was that he didn't touch the mowing machines or the harness for two weeks.

Hearn was gone most of the time. When he got back, he started to curse Sam for his laziness. Sam had never worked as hard in his life as he had for those weeks. His back was giving him hell, and he hadn't been able to straighten up for three days; so when Hearn began his tirade, Sam threw his hoe down and headed for the house.

"Hold on!" Hearn ordered. "Where are you going?"

Sam turned and faced Hearn. He said, "I don't know what you're aiming at, Vic, but I've had enough. You need two men here and you know it. Well, I'm not two men."

"You're not for a fact," Hearn agreed. "You're not even one man."

Sam started toward the house again. Hearn ran after him and grabbed him by the shoulder. "You stand still while I'm talking to you, old man."

Sam stared at him bitterly. " 'Old man,' " he repeated. "I guess the last two weeks have made an old man out of me, all right. You don't want an old man on H Ranch, so I'll pull my wagon around to the front of the house and load up tonight. I'll be gone by morning."

"You won't do it, and don't try to bluff me. Clara won't go."

"Then she'll be staying here alone," Sam said. "I'm going." He put a hand to his back and straightened up, grimacing as pain shot along his spine. "I came here on Clara's account. I guess I didn't know you, Vic, but I do now. I reckon it's time I was finding out how Clara feels about me."

"You still don't know me." Hearn's expression was not pleasant as he looked at the smaller man. "All right, Sam, see if you can get at those mowing machines next week."

Hearn strode to the barn. Sam returned to his hoe, picked it up, and went back to work. He should leave. He wasn't sure how that knowledge came to him, but it did, a strange warning that he could not explain; but it was as real as any knowledge that had ever been in his mind. He wouldn't go, though. He knew that. Not unless Hearn forced him to. The truth was, and he faced it honestly, he couldn't bear being separated from Clara, and he just wasn't sure she would go back to the Deschutes with him. He thought she would. She'd try to change his mind, but when she discovered she couldn't he thought she'd go.

Still, he wasn't sure of her, not as sure as a husband should be of a wife. It had never been that way before and it worried him. Even if she did leave, nothing would ever be quite the same between them. She would think, and maybe she would say, that he'd had something good dropped into his lap and he'd refused it. Sam realized dismally that she had a right to believe that because she had never seen Hearn as he had. Or as Hugh must have seen him. It was plain that Hearn did not want Clara to know him as Sam knew him. When he was with her, he was very careful to retain the veneer of amiability which he wore so easily.

That evening Hearn came to the little house after supper. He had not seen Clara for a week, but he hugged and kissed her as

177

if he had been gone for a year, leaving Clara flustered but pleased with his show of affection. She thought it was because they had been separated so long, Sam told himself, and he was happy to have her here. If it was true, it was only part of the truth, but Sam was not sure in his mind what the full truth was. He needed Hugh, needed him desperately, for Hugh understood things like this.

"Sit down, Vic," Clara said, "I'll get you a cup of coffee."

"No, I just got up from the table," Hearn said. "Jean had a good supper tonight." He drew a cigar from his pocket. "How are you getting along with Jean, Clara?"

"All right, I guess, but she isn't very friendly. Why don't you let her go, Vic? I could keep house for you as well as she does, and you could save what you pay her."

Hearn nodded as if he had already thought of it. "Maybe I will." He lighted his cigar and pulled hard on it a moment, glancing at Sam. "The grass is coming fine. We'll have a good hay crop. Looks like we'll be starting in about a week or so."

Sam said, "The mowers will be ready."

"We're short on horses," Hearn said. "I'm going to Canyon City tomorrow and see if I can't pick up some."

"You might as well use our team," Clara

said. "Hadn't he, Sam?"

"Might as well," Sam agreed.

Hearn rose. "I need more than one extra team with a crop as big as this one. Well, I'd better get to bed. It's a long ride to Canyon City."

He had stayed only a minute or two. Why had he come? That night Sam lay awake a long time, wondering what his reason had been. Had he just wanted to kiss Clara? Sam was alarmed by the thought, not so much because it might be true, but because of what it showed Sam about himself. He was jealous. It was a new emotion to him, and he didn't like it because he was ashamed. He thought about it a great deal during the next few days. Now that the full devil of suspicion had been aroused in him, he could not forget it. He had no doubts whatever of Clara. She would never think of Hearn as anything but a brother.

Rains during the last days of June and the first of July gave Sam a reprieve so that he was able to give his time to the preparations for haying. Hearn was gone until the afternoon of July 3rd. He seemed pleased with the work Sam had done.

"We'll start cutting on the fifth," Hearn said. "I'll round up the crew tomorrow. I've got another job for you, Sam. We'll go to the house and I'll tell you about it."

Sam walked to the little house with Hearn, feeling more uncomfortable than ever with him. He watched glumly while Hearn kissed Clara, then Hearn said, "I got onto some horses over on the Malheur. Clara, I want you to throw some grub in a sack. Sam, go saddle up. If you start out now, you can reach Juniper Springs by dark. Then it's an easy morning's ride to Max Knettle's ranch."

"But it's four now . . ." Sam began.

"Several hours till dark," Hearn said briskly.

"I won't get back in time to start haying."

"It'll take a day or so to get organized. You'll be back in time." Hearn handed Sam a money belt. "There's a thousand dollars. You probably won't need that much, but I want you to buy all the horses he's got that look good. They're broke, so we won't have to waste time with 'em after you fetch 'em home."

"You might not like the horses I'll pick," Sam said. "I don't think I can . . ."

"Sure you can," Hearn said. "You're a good judge of horse flesh."

"I'll fix your supper," Clara said. When she saw that Sam was hesitating, she added, "He's showing his confidence in you, Sam. I

180

think you should be pleased."

Sam left the house without a word. As he caught and saddled his horse, he could think of only one thing. He'd be gone for at least two nights, and Hearn would be here with Clara. Funny how he had changed in the month he'd been here, Sam thought. He had left them together when he'd gone to Prineville without having the slightest doubt.

He rode to the house, tied the sack of grub behind the saddle, then listened to the directions Hearn gave him. He kissed Clara, not wanting to go, but unable to think of a good reason for not going, a reason that would sound logical to Clara. He looked at her for a long moment, thinking that this month on H Ranch had been good for her. She looked happier and younger than she had for years.

He mounted and rode away, looking back only once to wave to her. She was still standing in front of the house. She would stay there until he was out of sight. She loved him. He had no reason to doubt her. But he hadn't, he thought. He never had. It was Hearn who worried him. Once Hearn had his grip on you, he twisted until you were ground into submission. Sam knew the man had a reason for sending him on this trip.

The logical move would have been to send one of his buckaroos. But no amount of thinking brought any answer to Sam. He'd find out in time, he told himself. Still, the uneasiness lingered in him and he wished he had left H Ranch days ago when he had come so close to doing it.

He found Juniper Springs at dusk just as Hearn had said he would. It was on the pass east of the valley, a cool, clear stream that broke out of the rocks below the road and disappeared down the side of the mountain. By the time he had made camp and eaten his supper, full dark had come. He sat beside his fire and smoked his pipe, listening to the coyote chorus that suddenly broke out from the rim to the south; then he heard someone riding toward him.

He had nothing to worry about, he told himself. Probably it was some buckaroo who had gone to town and was headed home. Or maybe a grub-line rider. For a time Sam fought his fears, feeling the pressure of the money belt around his middle. That was the reason he was afraid, he told himself. He had never had so much money on him in his life. Now that it was too late, he wished he'd made camp farther away from the road. A few minutes later the rider appeared out of the darkness. For a moment

Sam stared at him in absolute disbelief, unable fully to grasp the fact that he was looking at Vic Hearn.

Hearn swung down, saying nothing until he walked to the fire. Then he said, "Give me the money belt."

Sam obeyed, beginning to tremble, for he saw a quality in Hearn's face he had never seen there before, a sort of wicked anticipation, as if he had finally reached a moment he had been enjoying in his mind for a long time.

Slowly Hearn's right hand moved toward the butt of his gun. Sam wasn't armed. There wasn't even a rock within reach. Frantically he dived for the fire, grabbed a chunk of burning wood and threw it at Hearn.

Hearn stepped aside, the chunk missing him by two feet. Then his gun was in his hand. Sam felt the bullet hit him in the chest, a great blow that slammed him back. As he fell, all knowledge and all feeling left him.

The last vestige of restraint broke in Hearn, and he kept firing until there were five bullets in Sam Moberly's broken body. Hearn ejected the shells and reloaded, then holstered his gun. He turned to his horse, stepped into the saddle, and rode back the way he had come.

Chapter 18

On the first day Hugh was able to ride, Frank Clemens took him to Billy Goat Pete's horse ranch in the pines north of the valley. "He's an eccentric," Clemens said, "but he's clean and he's a good cook. You can put up with him for a while. It's the best place for you to go because it's the safest." Clemens grinned. "Besides, he doesn't like Hearn, either."

Hugh found that Billy Goat Pete was indeed an eccentric. He was a skinny old man, seventy or over, but he was spry and active. His laugh did sound exactly like the baa of a billy goat, and he even resembled one with his long face and skimpy white beard.

Hugh liked the old man from the first. Pete kept his one-room log cabin reasonably clean, and his cooking, although monotonous because it had little variety, was palatable enough. He loved to talk, and because he told a story well Hugh was a good listener, a fact which endeared him to Pete. The old man had been all over the West and up into Canada and deep into Mexico as well. He didn't query Hugh about his past, mostly because he was only interested in his own, and that suited Hugh. But Pete never talked about the one thing in which Hugh was most interested, his reason for disliking Hearn.

Hugh stayed with Pete through the month of July, regaining his strength slowly, and taking a little more exercise each day. But in spite of his care, his side still bothered him, and he knew it would be a long time before he was able to handle himself as well as he had before his beating in the H Ranch barn. He spent some time practicing with his gun every day, and found he was as fast as ever; but he knew that if he were forced into any sort of rough-and-tumble fight he wouldn't last long. Not that it worried him. Next time it would be with guns, and that was the way he wanted it.

He fastened his hatred on Hearn, not on Oscar Phipps or Shagnasty Bob or the others. Still, he knew that the instant he met any or all of the men who had beaten him there would be no parleying. It would mean sudden gunsmoke.

Clemens rode from town on an average of

twice a week to see him, and Ellie came occasionally. He told them it wasn't necessary, but they seemed to want to come, and he welcomed their visits, Ellie's especially. The more he saw of her, the more he realized she was a pretty girl with pride and dignity; and she never indicated in any way that he owed his life to her.

Hugh was in love with Ellie before he realized it. He had never been in love before, and he didn't know quite what to say or do. He wanted to tell her how he felt, but when he thought about what lay ahead he knew he couldn't. If he lived, he would tell her; if he didn't, it was better that she didn't know. So, as the weeks passed, the relationship between them became a little strained.

On two occasions H Ranch buckaroos rode past Billy Goat Pete's place. Both times Hugh saw them and stayed under cover. They were not men he knew, and he had no quarrel with them, but the guiding thought in his mind was that he didn't want Hearn to know he was in the valley until the time was right. If these men recognized him, they'd take the news to Hearn. Even if they didn't know him, they'd see he was a stranger, and Hearn would investigate.

Late in July the hay crew worked into the north end of the valley, and although they were some distance from Pete's cabin Hugh kept out of sight. He could hear the steady clatter of the mowers; he watched them move across the flat in a carefully spaced formation, and he wondered how his father was making out, supervising an operation of that size. Someone else must have handled the job in the past. Now that someone, whoever he was, was out of a job. So there was bound to be jealousy, and therefore trouble, and he wondered how his father would handle it.

As Hugh's strength returned, his impatience increased. When Clemens rode out on an afternoon early in August, Hugh announced he was going back to town with him. For a moment Clemens looked at him steadily, offering no argument, his broad face showing his concern. Then he walked to a pine tree that grew in front of Pete's cabin and, sitting down, leaned against the trunk.

"What are your plans, Hugh?" Clemens asked.

Hugh was surprised. He had been geared for an argument, but this was a question, and Hugh wasn't prepared for it. Finally he said, "I don't know. I've thought about it until I'm almost crazy, but I haven't come up with anything. I thought I'd stay with you, or go to the hotel. Sooner or later Hearn will show up. Then I'll kill him."

Clemens filled his pipe. He said mildly, "Seems simple enough."

Hugh was irritated because Clemens, in his indirect way, had put his finger on the fallacy in Hugh's thinking. It wasn't simple. It was unlikely that Hearn would come to town by himself. Bucking the kind of odds Hugh would have to, the chances of his doing the job and coming through alive were slim. He had no desire to give his life in exchange for Hearn's. Too, there was his certainty that his mother would not understand his killing Hearn.

"All right," Hugh said as he rolled a cigarette. "You've lived with this for a long time. You tell me what to do."

"I can't." Clemens struck a match and sucked the flame down into the bowl of his pipe. "It's true I've lived with this situation a long time — four years, to be exact. I don't know any more about what to do now than I did then." He pulled on his pipe a moment, then asked, "You know why I feel the way I do? Why it's personal with me and not just a matter of pride the way it is with . . . well, Pete, for example."

"No, I don't," Hugh said. "Not exactly."

"Let's start with Pete," Clemens said.

"Most folks in the valley are like him. They make a living here. If they are to go on making it, they know they've got to get along with Hearn or have trouble. Pete's found out he can sell horses to H Ranch, but at Hearn's prices. Because he knows he's getting the dirty end of the stick, he's sore, but do you think he's sore enough to pick up a gun and fight?" Clemens shook his head. "No, he'll cuss. That's all. Just cuss."

"I had thought of seeing every man in the valley and trying to organize them, but I suppose they're all like Pete."

Clemens nodded. "Men will fight if and when they have a cause. The men who live around here are no different from other men. They're not cowards, but they're not heroes, either. Bob Orley. Dutch Myers. Daugherty. Ira Dunn. Pete. All the same. If you went to them, you could tell them that in the eyes of Vic Hearn they are chattels, that Hearn denies them the inalienable rights of free men. So, you'd say, let's get killed because we have a great principle that is at stake. What do you think they'll say?"

"All right," Hugh said. "I know what they'll say. That puts it up to me, I guess; but I'm not waiting four years."

"Just a minute." Clemens held up a hand. "It's true I've waited four years. I'll tell you

189

about my case. It's not easy to talk about and it's not a pretty story, but I think you should hear it. Four years ago I fell in love with Jean Phipps. She was sixteen. Just a girl, quite slender then, and almost as pretty as Ellie is now. Her father ran one of Hearn's ranches south of the valley. He has a number of small spreads in the sagebrush which don't pay but help keep other cowmen out. I went to see Jean as often as I could. I think she loved me. I had every reason to think she did. I planned to ask her to marry me, but before I did Hearn fired his foreman. I don't know why, but I do know he hired Oscar Phipps. Apparently Jean was part of the deal. She started keeping house for him."

Clemens took his pipe out of his mouth and studied it. Then he went on: "When Jean went there, I'm sure she was a good girl. Perhaps I'm fooling myself, but I'm convinced she was. I have no way of knowing what was said between Hearn and her father. Perhaps Hearn paid for her the way a man pays for a woman in a pagan country. Or perhaps it was a tacit agreement, with Phipps getting the best job in the valley. Jean is well paid, too, I suppose. I haven't talked to her since then. I'm not allowed to go out there, and she won't talk to me when she comes to town."

Clemens knocked his pipe out and put it into his pocket. "I lost the only girl I ever loved. Jean lost her innocence and her decency. Oscar Phipps lost his self-respect. He's part of Hearn's organization now, and he's big and important, but look what it did to him. Four years ago he wouldn't have had a part in beating you up. The same thing has happened to all of them who worked for Hearn, from Shagnasty Bob on down the line."

Clemens looked across the valley toward where the southern rim was lost in the August haze. He went on, his voice expressionless, "I guess the part that hurts most is the fact that Jean doesn't care any more. I'm sure she doesn't. I can tell by looking at her. He's made her into a prostitute. A harlot. A whore. Call her anything you want to, but that's what she is. She doesn't care. By God, Hugh, she just doesn't care! Is there anything worse than that? Anything?"

Hugh didn't answer. Now he had some idea of the bitterness that had been bottled up in Clemens for four years. Hugh knew how he would have felt if it had happened to Ellie. Not that she was like Jean. But how could he tell what she would be today if he had not been in the hotel that night early in

June and stopped Hearn? He remembered Ellie saying that Hearn was a man women first hated, then loved. Ellie had said she would kill Hearn. But perhaps Jean had said that, too, at one time. Hugh went into the cabin and packed the things he had brought from town, then told Pete he was leaving. When he offered to pay for his keep, Pete was insulted. "You was company for me," the old man said. "If you don't come back out to see me, I'll be mad. You hear? Mighty damned mad."

"I'll be back," Hugh promised.

There was little talk on the ride to town. Hugh kept asking himself what he would have done if he had been in Clemens' place, if it were Ellie instead of Jean? He wasn't sure. He knew Clemens was no coward. There was a purposefulness about the schoolteacher that told him Frank Clemens was a man he could count on, and yet he was sure he could not have held back as Clemens had.

Dusk had fallen by the time they reached town. They stabled their horses in Clemens' barn, then went into the house where Clemens pulled the shades before he lighted a lamp. After he had started a fire in the kitchen range, he turned slowly to face Hugh. "I hope you don't think I'm a coward," Clemens said. "I'm not. I'll give my life for victory, but not for defeat. I hope you can see this the same way."

"I don't know about that," Hugh said, "but I sure never figured you for a coward."

"Here's the way it looks to me," Clemens said. "Men live by selfish motives, to achieve creature satisfactions: food to fill their bellies, a roof over their heads, clothes to wear, women to sleep with, perhaps a position of importance. But all of them have fears and hates. Those are the emotions which stir all men to action, but only when they are aroused. I have been convinced that sooner or later Vic Hearn will do something to trigger off the hate the valley people have for him. When it happens, there will be no stopping them."

"But how long can you wait?" Hugh asked. "Can you go on and on?"

"No, I can't," Clemens said. "I've been fighting it for weeks. I can't fight it much longer." He turned to the stove, filled the fire box, and then faced Hugh again. "There's something you've got to know. Ellie's been after me to tell you, but I wanted to put it off as long as I could. Before I tell you, promise me that whatever you do you'll let me help you. I deserve that."

Hugh nodded, thinking he could safely make that promise. He said, "All right."

"Your father was murdered during the last of June. We don't know who did it. He was found near the road at Juniper Springs. We didn't hear about it for a long time. They buried him at H Ranch. No one from town was there for the funeral."

Hugh sat down at the table. He didn't intend to. His knees simply gave way under his weight. He stared at Clemens, unable to think coherently; then it came to him that his father's killing had been inevitable. He should have known from the first. "It's up to you and me, Hugh," Clemens said. "Will you keep that promise?"

Hugh nodded. "Unless you want to go on waiting."

"No," Clemens said. "I can't wait any longer. I wish I could, but I can't. We've got to destroy him, Hugh. Some way we've got to destroy him!"

Chapter 19

Hugh could not fully comprehend what his conscious mind kept telling him was true, that his father was dead, Sam Moberly who had never harmed anyone, Sam Moberly who had loved his wife so much he had come here to work for Vic Hearn who had killed him.

For a wild, terrible moment Hugh hated his mother, holding her responsible for his father's death. Yet, when the bitter moment passed, he knew he could not blame her. If there was any blame, it was on him. From the moment he'd heard his parents were moving here, he had known that only trouble would come of it, only unhappiness for his mother. He had told himself he could not stop the move, and yet he should have, even if it had meant killing Vic Hearn. His mother would have hated him, but that would have been better than letting the situation go to its ultimate end — the murder of his father. Frank Clemens glanced at him anxiously. Finally he said, "I don't know what you're thinking, Hugh, but I'm hoping you don't figure on jumping the gun."

"Who found him?"

"Whitey Mack and Curly Holt."

"Hearn killed him," Hugh said, "and then sent them two bastards out to bring him in."

Clemens nodded. "Could have been that way, but there's no proof. The story is that Mack and Holt had been over on the other side of Juniper Springs looking for strays and were on their way back to the ranch when they saw your dad lying beside his campfire. It was out, but his stuff was still scattered around and his horse was there."

"The law?" Hugh demanded. "Doesn't anyone even pretend there's law in this valley?"

"Hearn makes a pretense," Clemens said. "The sheriff is in Canyon City, but he's a long ways from here on the other side of the Blue Mountains. He never comes to the valley. Even a murder wouldn't make him ride this far. It wouldn't make any difference if he did. He's Hearn's friend."

"You said once that the people in the valley would fight if something happened that was bad enough," Hugh said. "Is Pa's murder bad enough?"

Clemens shook his head. "I don't think so. They didn't know him. Even if they had, we'd need absolute proof that Hearn did it. Then if they thought it might happen to one of them . . ." Clemens spread his hands. "I don't know what it will take, Hugh. Maybe nothing could make them fight. Sometimes I get the feeling that after a man swallows his pride long enough, he doesn't have anything left inside."

Hugh stared at the teacher, his hands knotted on his lap; suddenly the tension broke, and all sense of logic, all restraint, was gone from him. He was conscious of nothing except that Vic Hearn had to die. He got up and kicked his chair back, and without a word started toward the back door. Clemens must have expected the move. He acted with startling speed for a man of his bulk; catching Hugh by an arm, he turned him around. "You can't go out there, Hugh!" Clemens said. "Not like this."

Hugh glared at the teacher, who was a full head shorter than he was. He tried to twist free, but could not. Frank Clemens was like a block of granite. Hugh raised his free hand to strike Clemens in the face, but the schoolteacher neither flinched nor relinquished his grip. Hugh dropped his hand.

"I'm not like you, Frank. I can't wait for four years."

Clemens' face turned red. "You're saying I've been too careful with my life. Well, I told you I'd give it for success, but not for failure, and that's what you're setting out to do. It's no good, Hugh. You've got too much to live for."

"What have I got to live for?" Hugh demanded.

"Your mother," Clemens said. "And Ellie. What do you think will happen to her if you're killed? Or if Hearn finds out she took care of you and saved your life?"

"All right, let go." When Clemens dropped his hand, Hugh said, "You're going to keep on saying that we've got to wait until he destroys himself. I tell you I can't wait, Frank. Can you understand that?"

"I can understand it," Clemens said. "Hugh, listen to me. Everything that happens to us, every event in life, is the result of something that has already happened. It's all cause and effect. This is the first time Hearn has murdered a man. It will finish him. Maybe not tomorrow. Maybe the day after tomorrow. But when the time comes, we'll know. It's like a delicately balanced rock. Just a little push will send it over the edge." Clemens turned away. "Go see Ellie, Hugh."

For a moment Hugh stared at Clemens' broad back as he stacked the dishes, then he went out into the darkness. He walked slowly toward the hotel, trying to think coherently, trying to be logical, but he discovered he couldn't. He had never faced anything like this before, the need to kill a man so strong in him that he could not hold back.

He was trembling when he went into the hotel through the back door, and sweat was running down his face. Frank Clemens could go or stay in town. That was up to him, but for Hugh Moberly there was no choice. He would see Ellie as Clemens had said, and then he would go to H Ranch.

He heard Ellie working in the kitchen. He stepped into the room from the hall, saying, "Ellie."

She was washing dishes, her back to him. She whirled when she heard his voice, her lips parted, her eyes wide, and then she said, "Hugh," as if she couldn't believe he was really there. She dried her hands on her apron as she ran to the dining-room door, closed it, and then went to him, quickly, without reserve, and threw her arms around him. Hugh pulled her to him and kissed her, and it came to him in that wild, sweet moment that he did have everything to live for. Clemens was right. He was crazy to throw his life away for failure. When at last she drew back, he said, "I love you, Ellie. I didn't intend to tell you until this was over, but I guess I just had to."

He tried to smile at her, but his lips were stiff, and he could do nothing but stand there and look at her and wish he could find the right words to say.

"I wanted to hear you say it, Hugh," she said softly. "I wanted it more than anything else in the world. Come over here and sit down. Are you all right? Are you sure you should be here?"

"I'm all right." He sat down beside the table. "Frank told me about Pa."

She bit her lower lip, glancing at him, and then said, "Hugh, I wanted to tell you before, but Frank was afraid you'd do something foolish. He said some men could wait, but you were one who couldn't."

"He's right," Hugh said. "I'm going after Hearn."

She whirled to face him. "You said you loved me. Does that mean you want to marry me, or is it just something to say?"

"Of course I want to marry you. We'll go back to live on Pa's place on the Deschutes as soon as I can get Ma. We'll take Ira with us. It'll be a lonely life for you for a while, but not for long. Pa always said the railroad would come. It will, inside a year or two, and then it won't be lonely."

"You think I can marry a dead man?"

"I don't figure on being a dead man. Not right away, at least."

"Oh, Hugh, what do you think will happen if you go after Hearn? Is it your mother you're worried about?"

"Partly, but mostly it's because there's no law here to handle Hearn. I've got to go!"

"And die." She shook her head at him. "I shut the dining-room door because some men were out there and I didn't want them to know you were here. As soon as Hearn finds out, he'll come after you."

"Maybe that's the way to do it," Hugh said. "Maybe I ought to send word to him."

She nodded. "But you need help. It's more than a two-man job. Frank Clemens is the only one in the valley the people will follow. I'm not sure they'll follow him, but they might if something happens that riles them enough. That's what he's been waiting on. Everyone in the valley loves him — everyone but the H Ranch crew."

Hugh rolled a cigarette. In the back of his mind there had always been a reluctance to take the fight to the ranch where his mother would see it and perhaps be endangered by it. But if Hearn came to town, even with some of his crew . . .

"Hugh, are you still thinking about your mother?" Ellie asked. When he nodded, she said, "If nothing has happened to her by this time, then it won't happen in the next few days. Don't you see that?"

He shook his head. "No, I don't. Not with Hearn." He motioned toward the dining-room door. "Who's out there?"

She hesitated. "It doesn't make any difference."

"Who's out there?"

She hesitated again, then said reluctantly, "Whitey Mack and a buckaroo named Slim Lee. They came in for supper —"

Hugh lunged out of his chair and threw the door open. The dining room was empty. He whirled back to face her. "They're not there!"

"They were about done when you came in," she said. "I guess they've gone across the street to the saloon."

"Who's Slim Lee?"

"His dad drives the stage between here and Prineville. Slim went to work on H Ranch about a year ago. He's just a kid, twenty or twenty-one, but he's big-headed like everyone else who works for Hearn."

Hugh strode through the dining room. She called after him, "Hugh, what are you going to do?"

He went on, not answering her, for now he knew exactly what he had to do.

Chapter 20

Hugh paused in front of the hotel, glancing along the street. The only lights were those in the hotel and in Dutch Myers' saloon. There wasn't even a lighted lantern hanging in the archway of Daugherty's livery stable. Two horses were tied at the hitch rack in front of the saloon. They'd be Whitey Mack's and Slim Lee's. The night was black dark, the starshine blotted out by heavy clouds. The rumbling sound of thunder came to him from the mountains to the north. He drew his gun from the holster and checked it. As he considered what he had to do, he realized that the problem was to keep from killing Slim Lee. The buckaroo must take Whitey Mack's body back to H Ranch if Mack forced a fight. That would bring Hearn to town. Whitey Mack was a hardcase just like Shagnasty Bob and Curly Holt. All three of them would die, and when they did some of the props would be knocked out from under Vic Hearn. That wasn't important, for Hearn wasn't a man who depended upon props. Any way Hugh looked at it, he knew he was bucking long odds. The question was how long they would be.

If Hearn brought his entire crew to town to find Hugh, the odds would be too great. Even with Frank Clemens' help, he could not fight fifteen or twenty men. That was why Ellie had said this was more than a two-man job. But at this time of year, the crew would be scattered all over southeastern Oregon.

Hearn was unlikely to pull all of his buckaroos in to hunt down any man, no matter how much he hated that man or wanted to see him dead. So it seemed to Hugh that Hearn would come after him with Shagnasty Bob and Curly Holt, and maybe another man or two who would be handy. That would be the kind of odds Hugh could handle.

As Hugh eased the gun back into his holster, Ira Dunn said from the shadows behind him, "Don't go over there, Hugh."

"Why not?"

"You aim to kill Whitey Mack, don't you?"

"If he wants it that way, I'll oblige him."

"Do you know what you'll start?"

"Yes."

The old man took a long breath. He said, "Hugh, you were born for trouble. I know your kind. I've seen them all over the West. They're never satisfied to let things alone."

"Your kind is," Hugh said. "No matter how bad things are, you'll let them alone. That's what's wrong with this valley."

"Yes, if it was left to me I'd let things alone," Ira agreed. "We've got a living here. It's the only security I've ever been able to give Ellie. You're fixing to destroy it, and we'll have to start traveling again."

"Security," Hugh said, and wondered if Ira fully understood the price Ellie would eventually have to pay if they kept it. Perhaps Oscar Phipps at one time had reasoned the same way. "You never have security with a man like Vic Hearn, Ira. Ellie and I love each other. We'll be leaving here before long and we're taking you with us."

"I knew it would come to that if you lived long enough to marry her," Ira said. "Then I don't see no reason why we can't go now."

"No," Hugh said, and stepped off the porch.

"Wait," Ira said. "We're like sheep, Hugh. All of us in the valley but Frank and Ellie. A herder takes care of his sheep. Are you and Frank going to be herders?"

"No," Hugh said. "It's time the sheep

grew some teeth of their own." Hugh went on across the street, and paused outside the batwings to look into the saloon. Bob Orley, the storekeeper, and Daugherty were playing poker with Whitey Mack and a slender cowboy who would be Slim Lee. Dutch Myers stood watching the game. Whitey Mack sat with his back to the door. When Hugh stepped inside, the batwings making a swishing sound behind him, Bob Orley looked up. He immediately laid his cards down and rose and moved to one side. Then Daugherty glanced at Hugh and did exactly as Orley had done. Myers followed, all three clearly indicating they wanted no part of trouble. Slim Lee sat across from Whitey Mack, facing Hugh. He remained motionless, looking at Hugh and apparently not knowing what to do. Ellie had said he was twenty or twenty-one, but he had a gawky, adolescent look about him that made him seem younger. "Stay where you are, Lee," Hugh said. "I don't want to kill you."

Whitey Mack had not looked around. Certainly the thought that Hugh Moberly would be here had never entered his mind. When a man was handled as Hugh had been, he ran and kept on running. But now the sound of Hugh's voice made Mack turn his head. Hugh felt like laughing aloud when he saw shock hit the man and paralyze him.

"It's a little different this time, isn't it, Whitey?" Hugh asked. "Nobody's holding my arms now."

Still Mack sat there, staring, apparently not frightened so much as he was surprised by Hugh's appearance. Finally he said, "I thought you were with Joe Pope a thousand miles from here."

"I figured you'd think that," Hugh said. "I'm going to give you a job. You're riding to H Ranch now, and you're telling Hearn I'm here."

"You keep pushing me and I'll kill you," Mack said. "That'll be pretty hard on your ma after losing your pa."

"Did you kill him?" Hugh asked. "Or did Hearn do it and send you and Holt out to bring in his body?"

"I don't know who killed him," Mack said. "Curly and me found him and fetched him in. That's all." He licked his lips, his pale eyes expressionless in the cone of light that fell from the lamp overhead. "You've got me in a bind, Moberly. A man can't draw his gun, sitting like this."

"Then get up if you're looking for trouble," Hugh said. "Step away from the table. Lee, don't move."

"Funny about men like you," Mack said. "You never have enough sense to stay alive. If I get out of this chair, you're a dead man. I'll give you ten seconds to walk out of here. Then keep going, mister, because Vic will be on your tail as sure as hell."

"Get out of the chair and get on your horse," Hugh said, "or get up and make your play. Either way, *move!*"

Mack remained motionless for an instant, as if not believing any man would talk that way to an H Ranch hand. Now, staring at the hard set of Hugh's face, he must have been convinced that Hugh meant what he said. He came up out of his chair fast, wheeling away from the table and facing Hugh. His hand swept his gun from leather and brought it level, the hammer back. A split second after Whitey's first move, Hugh drew, a swift, sure movement that was the result of a natural facility and countless hours of practice. He shot Mack through the chest before the ranch hand could pull the trigger of his gun. Whitey was knocked back by the bullet and spun partly around, then he broke at knees and hips and spilled at full length on the floor. Slim Lee was on his feet reaching for his gun when Hugh threw a shot in his direction, splintering the top of the table. "I told you to sit pat! Put your hands in front of you. Palms down!"

Lee obeyed, his face shiny with sweat that had suddenly broken through his skin. He said, "You're a dead man, Moberly. Vic won't let this go." He tried to sound tough, but it didn't come off. He was a badly scared kid, nothing more.

"Myers," Hugh said. "Take a look at Mack."

The saloonman hesitated, glancing at Daugherty, then at Bob Orley. "I'm not having anything to do with —"

"Move, damn it!" Hugh said. "If he's dead, help Lee get him on his horse."

Myers obeyed then, kneeling beside Mack and feeling his pulse. He said, "He's dead."

"Then get him out of here. Lee, lay your gun on the table. Move slow. All right, that's it. Now give Myers a hand."

Lee rose. He took Mack's feet while Myers lifted his head and shoulders, and together they carried the body outside and tied it face down across his saddle. Hugh said, "Get on your horse and travel. Tell Hearn who did it."

Lee mounted, then looked back at Hugh standing in the lamplight that fell through a saloon window. He was scared and bitter, perhaps terrified at the thought of what Hearn would say to him for not taking up Whitey Mack's fight. Suddenly Lee began to cry. He wiped a hand across his eyes, then he yelled, "By God, I'll tell him, all right! He's in Winnemucca now; but I'll tell him and he'll get you! He'll get you, I tell you!" Lee rode away, leading Mack's horse. As Hugh turned toward Myers, the saloonman said, "He's right. Hearn *will* get you."

"Come inside," Hugh said. Myers shrugged and stepped through the batwings. Daugherty and Bob Orley had turned to the bar and poured stiff drinks. Hugh said, "Hearn killed my father. Frank Clemens says the law won't touch him, so that leaves it up to me."

Myers reached for a bottle and drank from it, then put it back on the bar. None of the three looked at Hugh.

"What kind of men are you?" Hugh shouted at them. "You've lived for years under Hearn's thumb. Is there any pride in you? Are you going to keep on sucking around after him the way you've been doing for the rest of your lives? Do you like yourselves, living the way you have been?" Still they said nothing. They wouldn't look at him. Clemens was right, Hugh saw. Any hope he'd had of getting help from these

211

men was gone. But he knew he'd never had any. Not any real hope. Ellie had said it was more than a two-man job, but there were just Frank Clemens and Hugh Moberly, and that only added up to two.

"Look at yourselves," Hugh said bitterly. He motioned to the back-bar mirror. "Go on, look at yourselves, if you can stand what you see." He walked to the batwings in long strides. When he reached it, Myers asked, "Moberly, do you know what you've just done?"

"You bet I know," Hugh said, looking back at Myers. "But what I'm wondering is whether *you* know what *Hearn's* done."

Chapter 21

Slim Lee took Whitey Mack's body to H Ranch and immediately caught and began saddling a fresh horse. Jean Phipps heard him, for she was unable to sleep. Actually, she had slept very little for weeks. Not since Hearn had moved Clara Moberly into the big house following her husband's funeral.

Hearn had been gone so much that Jean had had no chance to talk to him, but jealousy and a sense of not being wanted had built a smoldering fury in her that had grown to the point where she had to have it out with Hearn. He'd marry her or she'd leave. When she heard Slim Lee at the corral, she thought Hearn had returned from Winnemucca. She slipped on her shoes and, putting on a robe, left the house. When she reached the corral, she called, "Vic."

Lee had just finished tightening the cinch and was ready to leave. He said, "It ain't Mr. Hearn, ma'am. It's me, Slim Lee."

"Where's Whitey? Didn't he go to town with you, Slim?"

"He's dead, ma'am. Hugh Moberly killed him. I'm going after Mr. Hearn."

"Yes, you'd better get Mr. Hearn," Jean said, and returned to the house. For a long time she sat by the window in her room, staring into the night. She had something to work with now, a sharp weapon she could use to slit Clara Moberly's throat if she knew how to use it. She wasn't sure she did. She could tell Clara that her son was in town and had shot and killed one of Hearn's best men. As soon as Hearn returned, he'd go after Moberly and hang him for Whitey Mack's killing.

She was certain Hearn had killed Sam Moberly. She could tell Clara that, too. The danger was that Clara wouldn't believe her. They hadn't spoken for days. By tacit agreement Jean worked in the garden and Clara kept house. When Hearn was gone and Jean had finished her work, she stayed in her room. Hearn had fixed a small storeroom just off the kitchen for Clara's bedroom, and she sought refuge there when she couldn't find anything to do. The two women might just as well have been a hundred miles apart.

Probably Clara wouldn't listen long

enough for Jean to tell her anything. No, there was an alternative, a better one. She'd threaten Hearn when he got back, tell him he had to get rid of Clara, or Jean would tell her the truth. It would work, she told herself. Hearn would do anything to keep Clara from knowing what had happened. Jean wasn't sure why, but she was convinced that it was so.

Jean slept better that night than she had for weeks, not doubting that within a couple of days Clara would be out of her life. Jean was confident that if she forced a showdown, Hearn wouldn't give her up. She should have done it a long time ago, she thought.

The next day she rode to the cow camp in Crow's Canyon and brought Shagnasty Bob and Curly Holt back to the ranch with her, leaving word for her father to come as soon as he could. Whitey Mack's body had to be made ready for burying; there was a grave to be dug and a coffin to be made. Shagnasty Bob and Holt rode with her, silent and dour, and she had the satisfaction of knowing that Hugh Moberly had only a few days to live. She hated him simply because he was Clara's son.

The next day wore itself out, but Hearn didn't come. Jean kept telling herself what she would say to him and how she would say it, rehearsing her speech in her mind, over and over. It was midnight before she heard him ride in. Another half-hour passed before he climbed the stairs. She hoped he would come to her, but he didn't, so she crossed the hall and opened the door of his room.

He was sitting on the edge of his bed, tugging at his boots. He glanced up, his face covered with stubble and dust. He was saddle weary, but she sensed immediately that there was something else, some tension or worry, that she had never seen in him before. She stood looking at him, vaguely disturbed, for she had always supposed he was above the fears of ordinary men.

"What do you want?" he asked, his voice surly.

"I wanted to talk —"

"Talk?" He shouted the word at her. "I rode my tail off to get back, and then, by God, a woman wants to talk! Get out of here!"

She stepped quickly into the hall and closed the door. She knew this was no time to force herself upon him, but she had to fight what was almost a compulsion to open the door and make him talk. It had been bottled up in her too long; it had to come out. But the morning would have to do, she told herself, and finally she turned and went into her room.

Now doubts flooded her. She had been so sure she could do what she wanted with him. He needed her. She'd given him four years, and there had never been a day in those four years when she had not hoped he would come to her and ask her to marry him, to raise her from her position of "housekeeper," the polite word that people used when they talked about her. She would have it out with him in the morning. She would never have a better chance to win.

With the first sign of dawn above the eastern rim, she pinned up her hair. Clara would be getting breakfast, and she had to talk to Hearn before he went down to the kitchen.

Hearn was dressing when she went into his room. He gave her a sour look, saying, "I'm going to have to put a lock on my door."

She shut it and placed her back against it. She said, "Vic, I want you to marry me. Today."

He laughed. "What'n hell makes you think I'd marry you?"

"Because we love each other, and because of what I've been to you for four years."

"Let's get a couple of things straight," he said. "I don't love you, and what you've been to me I could have bought from a dozen women. Now get out of here!"

She felt cold, so cold she shivered involuntarily. She was beaten before she made her threat, and she wondered why she had ever thought she could bully Vic Hearn into anything. But she didn't move away from the door as she said, "Then I'll tell your Clara that her son is in town and that he killed Whitey Mack. I don't think you want her to know that. Or that you're going to kill him the way you killed her husband."

He rose from the bed and stood staring at her, his face shadowed because the lamp on the bureau was behind him. This was the Vic Hearn she had admired and loved, the great and powerful Vic Hearn who rolled over anything and everything in front of him, smashing those who opposed him. This time she was the one to be smashed, and she was sick with the knowledge that he had meant it when he'd said he could have bought from a dozen women all that she had been to him. "Pack your things," Hearn said. "I'll have Slim take you to town in a buckboard. You're getting out of here before you tell Clara anything."

She was trembling as if she had a chill.

She had been wrong. She didn't want to give him up. If she could hold him, even a small part of him . . . She cried out, "What is there about Clara that makes you feel this way? She'll never have you!"

"She'll have me," he said. "Did you ever know of anything I wanted that I didn't get?"

"But why has it got to be Clara?"

"I'm going to marry her," he said. "I'm going to leave this country and move to Portland. You think you're the kind of woman I'd take with me as my wife?"

"You think Pa will stay here and run your outfit when you're gone?"

"He's fired, too. I can hire a dozen foremen as easy as I can find women like you." He walked to her. "I'll tell you why it's got to be Clara. I never felt like a brother to her. In time she'll quit feeling that way about me. Clara's the only woman I ever wanted that I couldn't get, and I'll marry her to get her. I'll buy her the best house in Portland. I'll get servants for her. I'll . . ." He stopped, and scowled at her. "By God, Jean, you're stupid!" He jerked her away from the door, opened it, and shoved her through it. "I'll give you ten minutes, and I'll break your damned neck if you're not ready."

He stomped down the stairs. She ran into her room and began throwing clothes into a leather suitcase, not doubting that he meant what he said. He would break her neck and fire her father.

She was downstairs in less than ten minutes. She heard the buckboard drive up outside; she heard Clara cross the dining room into the parlor just as Hearn walked in through the front door. She turned to Clara, saying impulsively, "Ask Vic why you're in this house and who killed your husband and who shot Whitey —"

She was talking fast, trying to say all she had to say before Hearn stopped her. She didn't know he had crossed the room until he struck her on the side of the head. She fell over her suitcase, her skirt flying away from her legs. She hit hard, hurting her shoulder. She screamed, but before she could say a word Hearn grabbed her by an arm and hauled her to her feet.

"I should have got rid of her like you wanted me to," he told Clara. "I fired her this morning. That's why she's gabbing this way."

He hustled her out into the cool morning air, the eastern sky bright with the sunrise. He said, "Slim, fetch her suitcase." He lifted her and slammed her down into the seat of the buckboard. "Keep your mouth shut. You savvy what I'm telling you? Keep your goddam mouth shut about the things you were trying to tell Clara. I told you I'd break your neck if you didn't, and I will."

Slim Lee came out of the house with the suitcase and dropped it back of the seat. Hearn stepped away, his gaze on Jean, his face contorted by fury. She had never seen him look that way before. He would kill her just as he had killed Sam Moberly. Lee drove off, and Jean, huddled beside him, continued to see Hearn's face long after the ranch buildings were out of sight behind them.

Chapter 22

Hugh was eating dinner with Frank Clemens when Ira Dunn came to the front door, calling, "Hugh."

"This may be what we've been waiting for," Hugh said as he rose.

Clemens nodded. "Hearn's had time to get back from Winnemucca."

Hugh left the kitchen and crossed the front room to the door. "What is it, Ira?"

"Jean Phipps is in the hotel," the old man said. "She's saying some terrible things. Ellie don't know what to do with her. She wants you to come over."

Hugh hesitated, wondering if he should tell Clemens, but he decided against it. He had no idea why Jean had left H Ranch, but he was sure that her presence in town would open old wounds she had given Clemens four years ago. "It isn't anything, Frank," Hugh called. "Ellie wants to see me."

"Go ahead," Clemens said. "You can finish your dinner later. I'll keep it warm."

Hugh got his hat and strode toward the hotel, Ira running to keep up with him. "Did she come alone?" Hugh asked.

"Slim Lee brought her," Ira said. "Quite a while ago. She's got a suitcase. Lee dumped it on the ground, let Jean out of his buckboard, then turned around and headed back. Didn't say a word. Jean came inside and got a room. She stayed in it till dinnertime; then she came downstairs and started saying things about your mother and Hearn."

Hugh stopped and gripped the old man's arm. "What things?"

Ira swallowed. "They wasn't nice. That's what worried Ellie. Jean sat in the lobby and kept saying 'em. There was people in the dining room and they heard. Ellie just couldn't make Jean shut up."

"What did she say, damn it?"

Ira got red in the face. "She said . . ." He stopped and swallowed again. "She said that as soon as your pa was killed, Hearn moved your ma into the house and . . . and that he's been sleeping with her ever since."

Hugh dropped his hand from Ira's arm and started toward the hotel on the run. It wasn't true. It couldn't be true. Hearn had baited a trap by sending Jean to town, hoping to get Hugh to come to H Ranch.

Well, it wasn't going to work. He'd choke the truth out of the woman and send her back to Hearn. He was glad he hadn't told Frank to come with him.

Apparently Ellie saw him coming, for she was waiting in the hall where he ran in through the back door. She was white-faced and scared, gripping both of his hands as she said, "I've done everything I could to stop her, Hugh, but she won't shut up and she won't go back to her room."

"I'll shut her up," Hugh said, and strode along the hall into the lobby.

Jean was sitting in a rocking chair, her hands clutching the arms. Her face was pale except for one cheek that was swollen and bruised. When she saw Hugh, she said, "Well, Moberly, I thought it was time you were showing up."

"I'm here." He stood facing Jean. Several people were seated behind him in the dining room, but he didn't look around to see who they were. "You want to tell me what you've been saying for anyone to hear?"

"Why not?" She leaned forward in the chair, her eyes on him. "Moberly, you're not any tougher than your pa, and he was a chicken liver if there ever was one."

Hugh's hands knotted at his sides. He had never in his life wanted to hit a woman as much as he wanted to strike Jean Phipps at that moment. He'd found it hard to believe that she was as bad as Ellie had said, but he had no doubts now. Clemens was lucky that he'd never married her.

Jean laughed, a jeering sound that brought Hugh's temper close to the breaking point. "You're supposed to be a gunfighter, Moberly. You can shoot Whitey Mack, but when it comes to Vic Hearn, who murdered your pa so he could sleep with your ma —"

Hugh grabbed her by both shoulders, pulled her to her feet, and started to shake her. "You're lying! Tell everybody you're lying, or by God, I'll shake your teeth loose!"

Ellie cried out, "No, Hugh, no! Hugh, stop it!"

She had hold of his arms. He let go and stepped back; Jean fell into the chair. Hugh rubbed the back of his neck, realizing that for a moment he had been crazy with a red, compelling fury he had never known before in his life. His sanity returned to him; he knew he could not afford the luxury of an uncontrolled temper. He swung around to nod at Ira. "Go get Frank." He turned to Jean and hauled her up from her chair. "I'm taking you to your room. Ellie, you come up as soon as you get done in the dining room. What's her room number?"

"Two," Ellie said.

Hugh pushed Jean up the stairs ahead of him, heedless of her screams and kicks. He shoved her into her room and on the bed. "All right, now you can talk until your tongue's sore. Did you have to spread your filth in front of everyone?"

The look she gave him was venomous. She said, "I had a job to do. I couldn't think of any other way to do it, and I couldn't think of any other man who might take care of it."

"What job?"

"I want to see Hearn dead."

Hugh sat down in the room's only chair. He rolled and lighted a cigarette, trying to make some sense of her words. Of all the people in the valley, Jean Phipps should be the last to want Hearn dead.

"Well?" she demanded. "Are you just going to sit there?"

"I'm listening," he said, "if you've got anything to say that's worth hearing."

"Hearn killed your father. Don't that make any difference to you?"

"I figure he did," Hugh said, "but can you prove it?"

"I didn't see him do it, if that's what you

226

mean, but I know he was gone from H Ranch the night your father was murdered. I know when he got home, too. He'd been gone long enough to have ridden to Juniper Springs and back."

Hugh blew out a cloud of smoke, his eyes not leaving her face. Finally he said, "That isn't proof."

"It ought to be enough," she said. "Right after the funeral your mother moved into Hearn's house. This morning I told him I wanted him to marry me. He said he was going to marry your ma. Take her to Portland and buy her a fine house and have servants and everything. He had to get rid of your pa if he was fixing to do all that, didn't he?"

Hugh nodded. "I thought he'd wait till the summer work was over."

Her lips curled. "You were fools to believe that talk about your pa bossing the haying crew. Every farmer in the valley would break his neck to work for Vic. He pays good wages and they all need the money."

Hugh thought that Hearn had sent Jean Phipps to town to trap him, hoping to make him so crazy with hate that he'd ride to H Ranch and get shot to pieces. He said, "I think you're lying. You're playing Hearn's game. He expects me to come after him and he's got some bushwhacker lying on the rim waiting to plug me the minute I show up."

She raised herself on one elbow to stare at him. She said in a low tone, "Moberly, you're a fool." Suddenly she lay back, with her eyes closed, and began to cry.

When Ellie and Clemens came into the room, he told them what Jean had said, then shook his head. "I can't tell whether she's lying or not. I've got a notion it's a trap. Maybe Hearn's trying to suck me out there just like we were figuring on getting him into town."

"She's not lying," Clemens said, and sat down on the edge of the bed. "Jean, has it been worth it?"

She had stopped crying. She looked at Clemens, not saying anything for a long while. Watching, Hugh wondered if she was thinking of how it might have been if she'd married Clemens and had never gone to live on H Ranch.

"No," she said finally. "It wasn't worth it. But it's no good to say that now." She looked at Hugh, her lips curling. "I don't like you. Why should I? You're Clara's son, and she's the one who's made all my trouble. But if it hadn't been her, it would have been some other woman. Maybe Ellie.

I know that now, but I didn't all the time I lived on H Ranch. It's like he told me. I'm not the kind of woman he could take to Portland to be his wife." She closed her eyes, her hands clenched beside her on the bed. "I've been wrong. Pa's been wrong, too. In this valley you're either part of H Ranch and you're important, or you aren't part of H Ranch and you're nothing. I never saw Pa as happy as he was the day he told me he was going to ramrod H Ranch and I was to be Vic's housekeeper. He didn't tell me what else I'd be. Maybe he didn't know. I've never been sure."

Suddenly she opened her eyes and looked at Hugh. "He ruined my life, and I'm not the first. Ellie can tell you that. He'll ruin your mother's life because he won't be satisfied with her after they're married. Once he's got something, he doesn't want it. He killed your father. He'll kill you if he can." She licked dry lips. "I thought I loved him. But I hate him more than I love him. He's got to die, Moberly. If he doesn't, he'll ruin the lives of a lot of other people. Can't you see that?"

"I saw that a long time ago," Hugh said.

"It's not as simple as you're making it, Jean," Clemens said. "The question is how and when to do it. I've wanted to kill him for four years. I knew it would end this way for you someday, but I didn't know how to save you."

She turned her face to the wall. "I'm not for you. I never was."

Even after all that had happened, Clemens would take her if he could get her, Hugh thought. He was the kind of man who would give his love to one woman, and only one.

Clemens rose. He said, "Jean, a person can always make a new life for himself if he wants it." He turned to Hugh. "It's time to ride to H Ranch."

Hugh shook his head. "No. Whitey Mack's dead, and Hearn knows it by now. He'll be along. We'll wait for him like we planned."

Ellie, who had been standing by the window, cried out, "Hugh, look!"

Three men were riding into town from H Ranch, Shagnasty Bob, Curly Holt, and Oscar Phipps. They rode slowly, eyes flickering from one side of the street to the other. They were prepared for trouble and they would get it.

Hugh turned to Jean. "Your pa's riding into town."

She sat up, frightened. "Don't kill him, Moberly! He's not to blame."

Without answering he turned to the window again. Watching the three men in the street below him, he had only one regret. Vic Hearn was not with them.

Chapter 23

Hugh turned to Clemens. He said, "Stay here, Frank." He walked to the door, nodding for Ellie to come with him. When they reached the lobby, he said, "Call Phipps over here. Just tell him Jean's here and wants to see him."

She gave him a questioning look, then moved to the door as Hugh glanced out of the window. He said, "Wait till they're ready to go into the saloon."

The H Ranch men reined up and dismounted, moving slowly and warily, as if expecting Hugh to appear. They tied their horses and stepped up on the saloon porch, Phipps trailing Shagnasty Bob and Curly Holt.

"Now," Hugh said.

Ellie nodded; then, standing in the doorway, she called, "Mr. Phipps, Jean's here and wants to see you right away."

All three men wheeled, hands dropping to gun butts. When they saw who had called, they looked at each other, redfaced, hands falling away from their guns. Shagnasty Bob said something to Phipps. The foreman shook his head and strode toward the hotel, not looking back at the others, who watched him a moment, then went into the saloon. "Go into the dining room," Hugh told Ellie.

She hesitated, her worried eyes on Hugh, then obeyed reluctantly. Hugh drew his gun, moved to the door, and stood beside it. The instant Phipps stepped into the room, Hugh rammed his gun into the small of the man's back.

"Hook the moon, mister," Hugh said. "After what you did to me, it would be a pleasure to give you two back bones instead of one."

"No need to kill me," Phipps said. "I can do you more good alive than dead."

"I'll bet you'd do me a lot of good," Hugh said. "Now get those meat hooks up."

Phipps lifted both hands. "I figured you were dealing when the girl hollered. That's why I told the other two boys to let me play the hand out. My way, Moberly. Not theirs."

Hugh lifted Phipps' gun from the holster and slipped it under his waistband. "Up the stairs."

"Moberly, you damned fool," Phipps said angrily, "I want to talk to you. What do you think I came over here for?"

"You can talk to Jean," Hugh said. "Or listen to her, which will be better. Now climb those stairs. She's in Room Two."

Phipps jerked his head around to look at Hugh. "Are you bulling me?"

"No. She's here. I'm telling you once more to go up those stairs, Phipps. I won't tell you again."

Phipps obeyed, taking the stairs two at a time. He plunged into Jean's room, apparently not believing Hugh, and stopped, staring at his daughter. She turned her head on the pillow to look at him, her face expressionless.

Phipps motioned savagely to Clemens. "Get out of here. I want to talk to Jean."

"We've got nothing to say to each other, Pa," Jean said flatly. "There's nothing more that anyone can do or say."

"Come on, Frank," Hugh said.

When Hugh closed the door behind Clemens, Phipps was still standing in the middle of the room looking down at his daughter. Hugh said, "Keep him in there." He handed Clemens the gun he had taken from Phipps. "Those other two came to town to get me, so I aim to see they get a crack at me. I don't want Phipps boogering up the game."

Clemens took the gun. "You fetched Phipps over here just to cut the odds down?"

"It helps, but mostly I want him to hear what Jean's been telling me."

"She's in torment," Clemens said. "All this time she's lived in fear of losing something she never had. Now she knows she'll never have another chance." He followed Hugh to the head of the stairs. "Sure you don't want any help?"

"Just keep Phipps in that room, even if you have to plug him."

"Hugh." Clemens put a hand on Hugh's shoulder. "Hearn has become a legend in this valley. I've always thought that if we could destroy the picture people have of him, he'd come tumbling down like Humpty Dumpty off the wall."

"How do you figure to do that?"

Clemens motioned toward the door of Jean's room. "You remember what Ira said about people being sheep? You told me. Remember?" When Hugh nodded, Clemens went on, "He's right. If we can get one sheep to make a break, others are going to follow. Phipps and Jean might be the ones. If they are, I say to use them."

Hugh put a hand to his face, remembering the slugging Oscar Phipps had given him in the H Ranch barn. He said, "Don't trust them. If he gives you any trouble, kill him. I guess you never killed a man. Well, you'll never find a better one to start on than Oscar Phipps."

Hugh swung around and went down the stairs. Ira Dunn was waiting for him in the lobby. "What are you going to do, Hugh?"

"I'm going to give Shagnasty Bob and Curly Holt a chance to earn their wages," Hugh answered. "There's something I want you to do. You've got a rifle?" Ira nodded, and Hugh added, "Get it. Don't let Shagnasty Bob or Holt come into the hotel. Kill 'em if you have to, but whatever you do, don't let them get their hands on Ellie." When Ira hesitated, Hugh raised his voice. "Damn it, can't you understand? What do you think Hearn sent those bastards to town for?"

"They're after you, not Ellie."

"Sure, and they know that one way to suck me into a trap is to get Ellie. Maybe you don't think much of me, but you must think something of Ellie."

"She's everything to me," Ira said bitterly, "but if what you've done gets her into trouble, I'll . . ."

"It's your job to see she don't get into trouble," Hugh said, and strode along the hall and out through the back.

Hugh turned toward the livery stable. This was his game. He had played it many times and in many places — a game that must always be played by ear because the opposition was never entirely predictable. When the odds were against him, as they were now, the trick was to use any help he could get, even if it was weak. In this case it was Daugherty, the weakest possible prop.

The liveryman was cleaning out a corral behind the stable when Hugh reached it. He said, "Come here, Daugherty." The man continued to fork manure into a wheelbarrow. Hugh said, "If I go in there, you'll come out with your heels dragging."

Daugherty jammed the fork into the ground and walked to the gate, his rheumy eyes touching Hugh's face briefly and then glancing away. "What do you want?" he asked.

"You know Phipps' horse?"

"Yes."

"Three horses are tied in front of the saloon. Phipps' animal is one of them. Leave him there. Fetch the other two. Just untie them and bring them over here."

A pulse began throbbing in Daugherty's temple. "They'll kill me. I won't do it."

"Then I'll kill you," Hugh said. "Which

237

way do you want it?" He took the man by the shoulders and shook him. "Can't you get anything through your head, you belly-crawling worm? I'm fighting for my life. Yours, too, in the long run, but that's something you'd never savvy. Now, go get those horses!"

Daugherty took one look at Hugh's face, then started toward the stable. He paused, looking back at Hugh. "What do I say if they see me?"

"Tell them I told you to get the horses. If they ask where I am, tell them you don't know."

Daugherty licked dry lips, the pulse still pounding in his temples. "What did you ever stop here for? Why'n hell didn't you keep on riding?"

"Go on," Hugh said.

He watched Daugherty go through the stable door and along the runway into the street, and he thought that probably everyone in Hearn's Valley had asked the same question. There was no answer to it, no answer that would satisfy Daugherty or any of them. They had their way of life and apparently they were satisfied with it, so they resented anything he did that disturbed it. More than that, he was making them look at themselves, and they probably resented that as much as anything.

Hugh stepped into the stable; he lifted his gun from leather, checked it, and eased it back. He watched Daugherty while he untied the horses and started across the street with them. He had almost reached the archway of the stable when Shagnasty Bob and Curly Holt ran out of the saloon. "What'n hell you doing with our horses?" Shagnasty Bob bellowed.

"Moberly made me get them," Daugherty answered.

Shagnasty Bob cursed and started across the street on the run, Curly Holt following. "Where is that bastard?" Shagnasty Bob demanded.

"How the hell would I know where he is?" Daugherty said. "I don't keep track of him."

He was in the stable now. Hugh said, "Come on. Run. Get 'em out of here!"

Daugherty obeyed. He was through the back door and out of sight by the time Shagnasty Bob and Holt appeared in the archway, Shagnasty Bob cursing Daugherty and threatening to break his neck when he caught him. Hugh had moved into a stall, but now he stepped into the runway, asking, "You boys looking for me?"

Curly Holt dived headlong into the nearest stall, but Shagnasty Bob went for his gun, standing with his thick legs spread just inside the archway. Hugh drew and fired, the sound a great explosion in the confines of the barn. He hit the big man, but he didn't put him down. Shagnasty Bob got off a shot that kicked up the litter behind Hugh. Hugh's second shot caught him squarely in the chest, the blow jolting him and knocking him back on his heels. He went down, slowly at first, like a great pine that begins to totter, then, gathering momentum, crashes to the ground.

Hugh lunged toward the stall to his left, knowing it had been too much to expect both of them to stand there and fight to the finish. It probably was a good thing for him Holt hadn't. Hugh's first shot had not put Shagnasty Bob down, and Curly Holt would have had time, if he was any good with a gun at all, to have finished Hugh.

Holt opened up with three shots that splintered the edge of the wall of the stall. He was panicky, Hugh thought. If he wasn't, he would have known he had little chance of scoring a hit that way. On the other hand, Hugh was a dead man if he went charging up the runway. But because he wasn't a man who could stay bottled up, he did the only other thing he could by vaulting across the manger into the narrow opening between the wall and the mangers. It was quick and violent and desperate, a gamble that Holt would count on him coming the other way along the runway. He plunged toward the manger of Holt's stall, yelling, "I'm coming after you, Holt!" He reached the manger as Holt wheeled. Holt took a snap shot, a wild one, the slug burying itself in the wall behind Hugh and above his head. When Hugh fired, Holt's head jerked back as if it had been pulled by a sudden tug, and he went on over and lay still in the straw. Hugh stepped out of the manger and rolled Holt onto his back. The bullet had caught him below his right eye and ripped up into his brain.

Hugh, his gun still in his hand, went on into the runway and knelt beside Shagnasty Bob. He was dead too. Hugh rose and holstered his gun, wondering what Hearn would think when he heard that two of his best men were dead. These were the hardcases he had used to help build the legend he had become, but Vic Hearn was not one to depend upon others. He believed in himself, and perhaps that was the real reason he had become a legend.

It occurred to Hugh that it would be better if Hearn didn't hear about what had happened to his men. When they failed to return by morning, he'd come to town to find out for himself. Walking to the back of the stable, Hugh called to Daugherty. "Don't send word to Hearn about this. Let him sweat." Hearn would come, all right, Hugh thought as he left the livery stable. He would come soon, and that was the way Hugh wanted it.

Chapter 24

When Hugh returned to the hotel, he called Clemens down from the upstairs hall and asked, "What's Phipps been doing?"

"Nothing. Just talking to Jean. They kept the door shut, so I couldn't hear what they said."

Ellie came out of the dining room. When Hugh turned to her, he was shocked by the worry which was so clearly reflected in her face. She leaned against the door casing, her shoulders slack. She said, "Hugh, Hugh, is this the way we're going to live?"

Only then did he realize that he was the cause of her worry. He went quickly to her and put his arms around her. He said, "No. Shagnasty Bob and Curly Holt are dead. Now Hearn will have to do the job himself."

For a moment all of her weight came against him, her hands clutching his shirt. She tipped her head back and looked at him, then at Clemens, who stood beside the desk, and finally at her father, who had just come into the lobby carrying his rifle.

"Three men are dead," Ellie said to Hugh. "Four, counting your father, and it isn't finished yet. Hearn's only one man. Will this go on and on because Hearn escapes punishment?"

For a moment no one tried to answer, then Clemens said, "Who's responsible for it, Ellie? Is it all Hearn's doing?" He motioned upstairs to the room occupied by Jean and her father. "Isn't Jean to blame for what she's done? And Oscar?"

"You're talking bosh," Ellie snapped. "Of course it's Hearn. If it hadn't been for him, and if he hadn't been the kind of man he is, Jean wouldn't have gone to live on H Ranch. She'd be married to you and be having your babies and . . ." She stopped, suddenly realizing she was hurting Clemens, whirled away from Hugh and disappeared into the dining room.

Clemens smiled wryly. "She's wrong, Hugh. Can we lay our sins on someone else because we're too weak to turn down temptation? Aren't all of us who are here in the alley to blame for what Hearn does? Because we've allowed him to live, we've let him go on doing what we call evil." He shook his head. "No, we can't be excused, Hugh. We tolerated it. Me. Ira. All of us.

244

And by tolerating it, we have indirectly blessed it."

To Hugh this was foolish talk, and he wanted to say so, but when he looked at Clemens he held his tongue. Frank was suffering the agony of guilt, holding himself responsible for what had happened to Jean. That was foolish, too, for Clemens was in no way guilty. Then — and it hit him with shocking impact — he realized that he had suffered in much the same way, blaming himself for his father's death.

"Frank, let's ride out to H Ranch now," Hugh said impulsively. "We can handle Hearn."

Clemens acted as if he hadn't heard. "What is evil, Hugh? We can't define it, can we? For what is evil in one case may not be evil in another." The wry smile came to his lips again. "There was a man once who asked what truth is, but no one answered him."

Clemens turned toward the stairs and was halfway to the top when Hugh called, "Frank, didn't you hear me? Let's go to H Ranch. You say we're guilty of letting things go. Well, let's not be guilty any longer."

Clemens looked back over his shoulder. "Wait, Hugh. I want to talk to Jean."

He went on up the stairs, and a moment

later Hugh heard him knock on Jean's door. Hugh turned to Ira Dunn. "What's the matter with him?"

"No one knows but him," the old man said. "He talks way up in the clouds like that sometimes." He leaned the rifle against the wall behind the desk. "We've all hidden behind our fears, Hugh. I know what you think of me and I'm ashamed of it. Frank's ashamed, too, but it's worse because he knows more'n the rest of us." Ira glanced into the dining room, then brought his gaze to Hugh's face. "With me it's been worry over Ellie. It's like I told you. This was the only time since she could remember that she'd had any security, and I didn't want her to lose it. Now it's different. You're going to marry her. Stay alive, Hugh. If you do, I won't have to worry about what happens to me."

"I aim to stay alive," Hugh said. He walked outside and sat down on one of the benches in front of the hotel.

Presently Clemens came back downstairs and sat down beside Hugh. "I asked her to marry me, but she said no. She wouldn't ruin me, she said. She claims she's soiled, she's no good. She kept repeating it. She'd just drag me down, she said."

"Give her time, Frank," Hugh said.

"I don't have time to give her," Clemens said. "Not any more."

Hugh said, "Let's go, Frank. Now."

Clemens shook his head. "No. Your mother's still there. We can't risk it. We set out to force Hearn to come to town and we will. He'll come. Today. Or tomorrow." He laid a hand on Hugh's shoulder. "It seems to me I've been walking through a heavy fog for four years, but now it's lifted and I know what to do. Ira and I will ride over the valley and ask everyone to be here in the morning. I'll get Billy Goat Pete to help. We'll have fifteen or twenty men in town by nine o'clock."

"What good will that do? You've always said none of them would fight until something big happened."

"Your father was murdered by Hearn," Clemens said. "Phipps confirmed it. Hearn told him he was the one who did it. What we've got to do in the morning is to prove to them that no man in the valley is safe if Hearn decides to kill him."

Hugh said, "Frank, I've waited because it seemed the right thing to do. Or maybe it was because you asked me to, but I . . ."

"Till morning, Hugh. That's all. There's something else I don't suppose you can understand, but I do and I think it's important.

All these people feel guilty for letting Hearn run like a mad dog in the street. They'll never be free of that guilt unless they kill Hearn or see him die and know what he really is. They must not go on believing he's the legend they've built up in their minds."

"Oh, hell!" Hugh said. "You're dreaming this up. All these people want is to be let alone."

"It's in their minds whether they know it or not," Clemens said. "They're guilty and they know it. Maybe it's the weight of fear, but whatever it is they've got to be free of it. They must see him in daylight. Now you stay here and look after Ellie."

Clemens walked into the lobby and talked to Ira a minute; then they left through the back. Hugh got up, torn by indecision. He'd waited too long. He ought to stop them, or go with them. But he knew Clemens, knew that once his mind was made up, nothing could change him. With Ira gone, Hugh could not leave Ellie alone in the hotel.

He sat down and rolled a smoke, thinking of Ellie's question, "Is this the way we're going to live?" It wasn't. He would give her the security Ira valued so highly. Then he considered his mother, who had made a bad trade and who must know it by now. To all intents and purposes, she was a prisoner on

H Ranch. He wanted to see her. He wished that Ellie could talk to her, get acquainted with her.

There should be many years ahead of them, good years they should be planning now. He thought of the guilt that Frank Clemens kept talking about, and he knew his mother must be suffering the tortures of the damned, blaming herself for coming here. Then he wasn't sure. Perhaps she didn't know yet why Sam Moberly had died.

Ellie came out and sat beside him. He held her hand for a time, neither talking, both feeling a closeness that was new and wonderful. At six o'clock Phipps was still upstairs with Jean, and Ellie asked Hugh to go to their room and find out if they wanted supper.

Phipps opened the door and stepped outside into the hall when he saw who had knocked. He said, "She's asleep. I don't want to wake her up."

"Supper's ready."

"I'll come down," Phipps said.

But after they were seated in the dining room and Ellie had brought their orders, Phipps only moved his food around on his plate. He looked like a sick man, Hugh thought. The foreman, who had been so big and confident, walking in Hearn's shadow, even trimming his black mustache so that it resembled Hearn's yellow one, now sat with his head bowed. He even seemed to have shrunk in size.

When Hugh finished his pie, Phipps looked up. "Clemens told me Shagnasty Bob and Curly Holt are dead. Whitey Mack's dead, too. There were four of us besides Hearn in the barn that night. I'm the only one left. Are you going to kill me?"

"Any reason I shouldn't?"

"No reason," Phipps said dully, "except that you don't cut down a tree by chopping off the limbs. I'm not even a limb. Hearn fired me this morning. You won't hurt him by killing me."

"Why did he fire you?"

"When he threw Jean out, he said I wouldn't want to stay. We've got to leave the valley." He glanced at Hugh, his mustache failing to hide the trembling of his lips. "It's a crazy thing, Moberly. I never felt better than I did the time Hearn asked me to ramrod H Ranch. It was the kind of job I'd been after all my life. He wanted a housekeeper, and asked me if Jean would work. I told him she would. I thought I was doing right for her."

Phipps wiped a hand across his face.

"After that I heard some of the stories about him and Jean. I figured it was just dirty gossip. I almost beat a man to death for saying in front of me what everybody else was saying behind my back. But maybe I didn't really care. If Jean didn't like what she was doing, she'd come to me. That's what I told myself. Maybe in time Hearn would marry her. I hoped he would, but now I know he never intended to."

Phipps clenched his fists on top of the table and leaned forward. "She just lies there, Moberly. Lies in bed and cries and talks about Hearn. She loves him, and now there's nothing left for her. He told her she wasn't fit to talk about your mother. He called her stupid. He said he could hire a dozen women to do what she's been doing. She's a nothing, Moberly. Just a nothing, and the hell of it is she didn't know it until this morning. She talks about killing herself. I'm afraid she will."

Hugh, looking at the man who had beaten him while two other men held him, saw only a weakling who had no faith, no hope, and no future. "You'd better watch her for a while," Hugh said as he got up from the table.

"I'll sit up with her tonight," Phipps said. "Maybe I can think straight tomorrow.

Maybe we won't leave the country like Hearn said. Maybe I'll stay and . . . and kill him. I ought to, Moberly. By God, I ought to!"

Hugh watched him walk away. After Phipps disappeared up the stairs, Hugh thought of Clemens' question. What was evil? There had been no question in Phipps' mind about his daughter's sleeping with Hearn as long as there was a chance they might marry, but now that she had been thrown overboard it was wrong, and Phipps was talking about killing Hearn. But he wouldn't, Hugh knew. He had taken Oscar Phipps' size the night Phipps had beaten him and he couldn't fight back, and nothing had happened since then to make him change his mind.

Hugh helped Ellie with the dishes. Other people came in and ate supper and drifted away. At eight o'clock she closed the dining room and sat for a time with Hugh in front of the hotel. Finally he asked, "When should Ira and Frank get back?"

"Midnight," she said. "Or sooner."

Hugh knew he would not be easy until Frank Clemens returned. He didn't worry about Ira, but he did about Clemens. There had been something strange about the man when he'd come downstairs after talking with Jean, something strange and haunting which Hugh felt but could not identify. The longer he thought about it, the more strongly he felt it, a growing fear that Clemens intended to throw his life away, maybe go after Hearn himself. Yet that wasn't logical, and Clemens was a logical man.

"Why don't you go to bed, Ellie?" he said. "I'll sit up."

He put an arm around her and pulled her hard against him; he felt her tremble as she asked, "Tomorrow, Hugh. What will happen?"

"I don't know," he said, "but it will be the end. I wish it was tomorrow now." He kissed her, then drew his arm away. "Go on to bed. You'll need your strength in the morning. Get some rest."

She left, and presently the lights of the town began winking out. The saloon. The livery stable. The houses that were scattered through the grass. Finally the only light left was the one in the hotel lobby.

He heard a horse come in about midnight, and a few minutes later Ira appeared, so tired he was barely able to walk. "That's the most riding I've done for a long time. I'm going to bed."

"Where's Frank?"

"Ain't he back yet?"

"No."

"Well, I sure don't know where he is. He went north, and was fixing to ask Billy Goat Pete to help him. He should have been here sooner'n me unless Pete wouldn't do it."

Ira went on into the hotel. After that the silence seemed to press down upon the dark town. A dog began to bark, and others took it up; then the racket died. At three o'clock Hugh gave up and went to bed; but he lay awake, staring into the darkness, worry, like a vicious little animal, eating at his heart.

Chapter 25

As long as Clara Moberly lived, she would never forget hearing Jean Phipps say, "Ask Vic why you're in this house and who killed your husband and who shot . . ." and Vic hitting her with his fist as if she were a man, knocking her sprawling over her suitcase, then pulling her to her feet and saying something about firing her. Then he'd shoved her out through the door and across the yard to the buckboard.

Clara turned and walked through the dining room and into the kitchen. She felt as if she had been shocked awake by having a bucket of ice-cold water splashed into her face, awakened from what had been a most pleasant dream. Now, with the dream gone, she kept seeing Vic's big fists hitting Jean on the side of the face; she kept hearing the solid *whack* of the blow that sounded exactly like the pounding of her hammer on a piece of steak she was preparing to fry.

Mechanically she went through the motions of setting the table and getting Vic's breakfast ready. He came in presently and sat down. He said, "Sorry you had to see that, Clara. I didn't intend to hit her, but damn it, there's nobody that makes me as mad as she does. If I'd had any sense, I'd have fired her a long time ago like you wanted me to."

Clara set a platter of ham and fried potatoes in front of him and poured his coffee. She kept her eyes averted. Firing Jean Phipps was one thing, but striking her and knocking her down was something else, something so terrible that no explanation on Vic's part would alleviate what he had done.

She stood at the stove with her back to him. He said, "Come to the table, Clara."

She turned slowly, knowing she had to face him sooner or later. She said, "I'm not hungry this morning, Vic."

"Oh, for God's sake," he said in disgust. "I'm sorry you saw something that was unpleasant, but you don't need to get worked up about it. We're both better off with Jean gone."

The questions that Jean had thrown at her before Vic stopped her kept running through her mind. He hadn't wanted Jean to ask them, but Clara knew that she must

256

ask them herself, and this was as good a time as any.

"Why am I in this house, Vic?" Clara asked, "and who killed . . ."

"All right, all right." He slammed his coffee cup down so hard it banged against the table. "What's the matter with you, Clara? Jean didn't want you here from the first, and you know it. She tried to make trouble and she was still trying after I fired her. That's why she asked those questions."

"You haven't answered them."

"I shouldn't have to," he said angrily, "but I will. You asked to come to this house after Sam was killed because you wanted to look after me. You said that, Clara. Remember?" She nodded, and he went on, "Well, you've done a good job of it, and it don't look to me like you'd forget it. Besides, I didn't want you living by yourself. I think about your comfort, too, you know."

She was ashamed of herself then. Maybe she couldn't blame Vic for losing his temper. Having Jean Phipps around was enough to make any man get angry.

"As for killing Sam, I told you I didn't know who did it and I can't find out," he went on. "I think it was some saddle bum who stopped at Sam's camp, and Sam made the mistake of telling him he was going after some horses and the fellow killed him on the chance he'd have the money on him. Maybe Sam let it slip that he was carrying a thousand dollars. All I know is that Sam was murdered, and I'm going to keep on trying to find out who did it. It was different with Whitey Mack. He was shot in a saloon fight. He had a chance to draw and he was too slow. As far as I'm concerned, that ends it."

It sounded logical and right. He'd simply lost his temper when he'd hit Jean. She said, "I'm sorry, Vic. I guess I was just upset."

"I don't blame you," he said. "Now sit down and have a cup of coffee with me."

She obeyed, watching him in silence until he finished eating. When he rose, she asked, "What about the garden, Vic? If I keep the house, I don't think I'll be able to . . ."

"I don't expect you to work in the garden. I'll get a farmer to attend to it. I won't have any trouble finding a man."

She sat at the table a long time after he left the house. She hadn't realized how much she'd miss Sam when he was gone. Now that it was too late, she could only blame herself for not knowing and not telling him how much she loved him.

If she could just talk to Hugh . . . If she could only hear from him and know where he was and that he was safe and well. But maybe she never would. He was a drifter. Vic had told her that repeatedly. He would never settle down. Vic had said once that Hugh was the kind who would get killed in a saloon brawl; perhaps she would never hear what finally happened to him.

Later in the morning she walked up the slope behind the house to the little cemetery where Sam was buried and stood beside Vic through the short funeral for Whitey Mack. She cried, not for Mack, whom she had known only by sight, but for Sam, because the service brought his death back to her with poignant sharpness.

She returned to the house and started cleaning. The house didn't need it, but she had to have something to do. This was the way it had been every day, for she could not sleep at night unless she was so worn out by fatigue that her brain was numbed.

Vic came in for dinner, and when he finished eating he said, "It was pretty hard on you, wasn't it?"

She nodded, looking down at her folded hands. "I couldn't help thinking of Sam. He came here because I wanted to, but if we had stayed on the Deschutes he would still be alive."

"Don't blame yourself," he said sternly, and came around the table and kissed her.

"You've still got me."

She reached up and took his hand. "And I'm thankful for that, Vic. I'm very thankful."

He acted as if he wanted to say something; then he must have decided against it, for he turned and walked out. She washed and dried the dishes, built up the fire, and heated the irons. The day was a hot one, as most days had been lately, and with the fire the kitchen was unbearable, but she kept at her ironing and finished it before she had to start supper.

When Vic came in for supper, he seemed worried. It wasn't like him. But maybe it wasn't worry. She couldn't be sure what was in his mind. There had never been any question about Sam. She had always known what he felt and what he thought. But it was different with Vic, and it had been from the day she had moved into this house.

Tonight she felt this difference more than ever, for he kept looking at her across the table, and she had the disquieting fear that there was something in his mind which shouldn't be there, something that was . . . unclean. She was horrified when that word leaped into her consciousness, but it was the right word, and she did not attempt to deny it.

Now that the door was open, other questions rushed into her mind, questions that yesterday would have been barred but that now raced through her mind and disturbed her as nothing had since Sam's death. Was this Vic Hearn the same man she had known as a boy, the Vic Hearn who had been raised with her and who had been everything a brother should have been?

He'd been sixteen then; he was forty now. Anything could happen to a man in twenty-four years, but she realized that she had been seeing Vic in her mind just as he had been when he was sixteen. He would never have struck a woman then as he had struck Jean Phipps, and suddenly she knew why she had felt this morning that she had been brutally awakened from a dream, a dream that had possessed her from the day Vic first rode into the farm on the Deschutes.

"I want to talk to you, Clara." Vic rose, and brought his chair around the table and sat down beside her. "You're alone and I want to look after you. Not the way it's been the last few weeks, but to really make you happy. I want to marry you."

"Marry?" She shrank back against her chair, staring at him, and for what seemed an endless moment she couldn't breathe. He might just as well have hit her with his

261

fist as he had hit Jean Phipps. She whispered, "Are you out of your mind, Vic? We're brother and sister."

"You know we're not, Clara. Not really." He smiled. "And I'm not out of my mind at all. I've waited what seems a reasonable time after Sam's death to say this, but I can't wait any longer. I want to leave the ranch this fall and move to Portland. I intend to give you the best of everything. You've lived from hand to mouth for years, Clara. It isn't right. You're a beautiful woman. You deserve the best, and you've never had it."

She started to get up, but he took her hands and forced her back into the chair. "I'm not asking you to do anything wrong. I tell you I want what's best for you. We can't go on living in the same house this way, you know. People would talk about you, and if they did I'd kill them, Clara. Believe me, I would."

He leaned forward, his eyes on her, his whole body gripped by a tension she had never sensed in him before. He went on, "Try to understand, Clara. You're the woman I want for a wife. I've got enough money to go anywhere and do anything we want, but it's more than that. I've always loved you, Clara. Not as a sister, but as a woman. Even back before you were married . . ."

She cried out, "Don't say it, Vic! Don't talk that way!"

She broke free from his grasp and jumped up. She would have run into her room if he hadn't caught her and, putting both arms around her, brought her to him and kissed her. It was a long kiss, a brutal kiss, and when he let her go he said, "You're no sister to me. You never were."

She whirled from him, ran into her room, and slammed the door. She propped a chair under the doorknob and put her hands against it, afraid he would force the door open and come into her room. There was silence then, except for the terrible hammering of her heart and the sound of her breathing. Presently she heard him leave the kitchen. She turned and fell across her bed, and then the tears came.

She didn't sleep that night. She didn't even undress. She rose and cleaned the kitchen, moving without conscious thought. She was a body, her hands and feet behaving as if they were guided by some mechanism over which she had no control. When she was done, she returned to her room and, putting the chair against the door again, lay down on the bed.

She didn't know what to do. She couldn't think clearly. Maybe she would be able to in the morning. She couldn't stay here. Maybe she would start walking when it was daylight. She didn't have any money. She had never worried about money, not even when they were broke. Somehow Sam had seen to it that she was never hungry, no matter how hard times were. She remembered Ellie in the hotel. She had been kind. Maybe Ellie would give her a place to stay, maybe even let her work for her room and board.

Sam? She rubbed her forehead, trying to think. No, Sam was dead. Hugh? She didn't know. Hugh would take care of her if he knew what had happened. She'd find him.

She never wanted to see Vic again. She never even wanted to hear his name. Hugh had not liked him. Sam had complained about him, too. But she had refused to listen. God have mercy on her. She'd brought Sam here to his death. There had been peace on the Deschutes. Poverty and hard work and loneliness, but there had been peace and love, and suddenly she remembered that Hugh had come back to them the day before she had left. Maybe if she and Sam had stayed, Hugh wouldn't have gone off again. But she couldn't bear to think of that now.

She was aware that it was dawn. The lamp on her bureau was almost empty. She got up, filled her smallest suitcase with clothes she knew she would need, and then put on her heaviest shoes. It was a long walk to town, but she could make it by evening. Leaving the suitcase in her bedroom, she took the lamp into the kitchen and put it on the table. She found a flour sack in the pantry, and dropped half a loaf of bread and some roast beef into it. As she carried the sack into the kitchen and was laying it on the table, she heard the back door open. She whirled, crying out in fright. It wasn't Vic, as she had thought, but a stranger, a short man so broad of shoulder he seemed almost grotesque, but he had a friendly face. Frightened as she was, she felt the genuine kindness in the man as he crossed the room to her.

"You're Mrs. Moberly, aren't you?" he asked.

"Yes."

"I'm Frank Clemens. I'm the school-teacher in town. Your son Hugh is my friend."

"Hugh. He's here?"

Clemens nodded. "Here, and very much alive, in case Hearn has lied to you about it. I've been waiting outside until I saw a light in the kitchen. I wanted to talk to you when Hearn wasn't around. We know he killed your husband, and Hugh will tell you how some of Hearn's men almost beat him to death out here in the barn the last night you saw him. I came to tell you, and if you want to leave with me —"

She heard the shot from the dining-room doorway, as deafening as crashing thunder. She saw Clemens knocked back and partly around by the impact of the bullet; then she saw him go down. From the way he lay on the kitchen floor, his hands slack, his mouth sagging open, she knew that he was dead.

She turned slowly. Vic Hearn was dropping his gun into the holster. He said, "I'm sorry you had to see this, but I couldn't help it. He came here to kill me. I'll get Slim Lee and we'll hook up and take the body to town."

Hearn walked to the back door, then paused and turned to Clara. "I guess you'd better come with me. Nobody is going to call me a liar about how it happened, but it might be a good idea for you to tell the folks in town that Clemens came here to get me, and I had to shoot him to save my life."

He went out, closing the door. She was

alone with Frank Clemens' body. She sat down and put her head in her hands, wondering if she would have the courage to tell the truth, and whether it would do any good if she did.

Chapter 26

Hugh woke at sunup after a short, troubled sleep. Frank Clemens had not returned. Hugh dressed and went out into the cool morning air. For a moment he stood beside the gate, staring eastward across the valley toward H Ranch, but there was no movement anywhere on the grass. He went on toward the hotel, walking slowly.

Frank Clemens was dead. Hugh had no idea why he thought so, but it was a strong feeling he could not deny. Oh, there were a dozen things that could have happened to keep Clemens from coming home. His horse might have gone lame. He might have decided to stay the rest of the night with some of his friends. He might have found someone in trouble and had stayed to help. Sickness, maybe, and had sat up the rest of the night to spell off the family.

Hugh's mind jumped from one possibility to another, searching for something that would allay his fears, but nothing was good enough. Clemens knew he would be needed in town this morning. He'd have been here hours ago if he were alive and able to travel. By the time Hugh reached the hotel, he was convinced he would never see Frank Clemens again.

Ellie had just started a fire in the kitchen range when Hugh came in. She turned to Hugh without a word, kissing him and holding him with fierce possessiveness, and for the moment there were just the two of them, finding strength in each other and therefore able to thrust aside the shadow of Vic Hearn which had troubled them with its darkness for so long. Then Ellie drew back and, looking up at Hugh, asked, "Frank?"

"He didn't come home."

Ellie turned from him and walked to the stove. Hugh thought, *She knows, too.* He sat down at the table. He had never felt this way about anyone before, but he had never liked a man as much as he had learned to like Frank Clemens. He had never leaned upon any man as he had Clemens; he had never owed any other man so great a debt.

Ira Dunn came into the kitchen yawning and rubbing his eyes. He saw Hugh and stopped. "Frank?"

"He didn't show up."

Ira took a long breath and shook his head. "Then he's had trouble." He went to the sink, pumped a pan of water, and washed his face.

Ellie looked over her shoulder at Hugh. "See if Phipps and Jean want breakfast, will you?"

Hugh nodded and climbed the stairs. Phipps opened the door to his knock and stepped into the hall where he saw who it was. "Ellie asked me to find out if you want breakfast," Hugh said. Phipps hadn't slept, Hugh thought. The foreman's eyes were bloodshot, his hair disheveled, his face covered with dark stubble. Now, looking at the man, Hugh thought there was no hope in him, no desire to live.

"I'll come down," Phipps said. "Jean don't want anything. She didn't sleep much. Seemed like she had to talk. Had to tell me all that Hearn had done to her." He looked at Hugh, utterly miserable. "How can a man do things like that, Moberly? And how can a woman love a man and still hate him so much she wants to kill him?"

"I don't know," Hugh said.

He went back down the stairs, Phipps following. When they reached the lobby, Hugh said, "Hearn will be here this morning, I'm sure of it. He'll want to know what happened to Shagnasty Bob and Curly Holt. What will you do when he shows up?"

Phipps gripped his arm. "You don't think I'd fight for that bastard, do you? After what he's done to Jean?"

"You might," Hugh said, "but I'll tell you this. If you make one wrong move, I'll kill you."

"I won't," Phipps said. "I reckon we'll be leaving town on the next stage. Nothing to stay here for." He wet his lips, then added with pathetic eagerness, "If you need any help, Moberly, I'll back your play."

"I won't need it," Hugh said curtly. "The only time in my life that I ever really needed help was that night in Hearn's barn, and I sure didn't get it from you."

"I couldn't expect you to forget that, I guess," Phipps mumbled, and went on into the dining room.

Hugh sat down at the same table with Phipps, and presently Ira joined them. Ellie served their breakfast, more nervous than Hugh had ever seen her. When she returned with the coffeepot, he put his arm around her, saying, "Quit worrying, honey. It's going to be all right."

"How can it?" she whispered. "Nothing can beat Hearn. He's always taken what he wants and he always will."

271

"No," Hugh said. "He won't always. Not after today."

He watched her as she returned to the kitchen. She wouldn't feel this way if Frank Clemens were here, he thought. She had said it was more than a two-man job. Now there was only one man.

After they finished breakfast, Phipps returned to Jean's room and Hugh helped Ellie in the kitchen. Presently farmers began riding into town, and Billy Goat Pete was one of the first. The townsmen, Bob Orley, Myers, Daugherty, and the rest, joined the farmers, surprised at the gathering and asking the reason for it.

Hugh stayed inside the hotel as long as he judged he could, clinging to the thin hope that he was wrong about Clemens, that the teacher would come riding in across the grass. This was the time when he should be here, to talk to these men who were his friends, men who trusted him and would listen to him. If there ever was an occasion when the valley men could be worked into a force to strike against Vic Hearn, it was now.

When Hugh knew he could delay no longer, he went into the street. Billy Goat Pete saw him and yelled, "Hugh, where the hell have you been? Just get out of bed?"

"Been waiting for Frank to show up," Hugh said.

"Didn't he get home last night?"

"No. I haven't seen him since he rode out with Ira."

"I'll be damned." The old man scratched his ear. "That ain't natural for Frank. He got me to carry the word to the boys in my end of the valley. Then he lit out the other way. Ridin' east, he was, the last I saw of him." He turned to the man next to him. "Know Ted Prentice, Hugh? And Ed Hall?"

Billy Goat Pete introduced Hugh to the rest of the men in the circle. Hugh didn't know them, but they'd heard of him. They shook hands, looking at him warily. They certainly knew he had killed Whitey Mack, and perhaps they had heard about Shagnasty Bob and Curly Holt. They didn't want to offend Hugh, but they didn't want to be friendly, either, for that might throw them on Hugh's side against Hearn; being careful men, they would take no such risk.

For a time an awkward silence held them, then Bob Orley said, "So you boys are going into the cattle business? Now what do you think Vic will say?"

"He'll raise hell," Ted Prentice said quickly, "but we ain't worried. If just one of us done it, he'd be in trouble, but Vic ain't gonna drop a loop on all of us."

"That's the trick," Pete agreed. "Frank Clemens has talked it for months. We all throw maybe a hundred dollars into the pot and buy a pool herd. It belongs to all of us. We hire a rider to look after 'em. Run 'em in the mountains in the summer and drive 'em down into the valley in the fall."

"We'll keep 'em in the north," Prentice added. "Vic don't own the valley and he don't need all of it. We wouldn't be bothering him none."

Dutch Myers laughed. "What brand of whisky you boys been drinking? Ain't anything I sell."

"Must be real tanglefoot to make you talk this way," Bob Orley said. "You'd better forget it. I know Vic better'n you boys 'cause I've been here longer. I've seen him handle deals like this, and it ain't a purty thing to watch."

"There's sixteen of us," Pete said. "Hearn won't do a thing if we stick together."

Myers laughed again. "Which one of you wants cows bad enough to fight?" No one answered. "That's what I thought. I say what Bob says. Forget the whole business." He jerked his head at his saloon. "Let's get out of the sun. I'll stand drinks for the bunch of you."

274

Myers started toward the saloon, Bob Orley and Daugherty falling into step with him. The farmers would have followed if Hugh hadn't shouted, "Hold on a minute! Frank didn't call this meeting just to have a drink. There's something a hell of a lot more important for us to talk about than running cows in the valley."

They turned to him, Prentice demanding, "What's that?"

"My father was murdered by Vic Hearn, but Hearn's walking around same as ever. Why? Because there's no law in the valley, no law but Hearn's. What are you going to do about that?"

They shifted their feet in the dust of the street uncertainly, no one meeting Hugh's gaze. At last Orley said, "You've killed three of Hearn's men. It's like you say. There's no law here but Hearn's. I figure he'll hang you for them killings. Take my advice, Moberly, and light a shuck out of town."

"You're Hearn's man," Hugh said contemptuously. "You'd crawl from here to hell on your hands and knees if he said to." He threw out a hand in a gesture that excluded Orley. "You boys didn't know Pa, so maybe his murder don't mean anything to you, but it ought to mean something to know that any of you can get the same and nothing will be done about it. Nothing!"

Orley's face turned red. "Hogwash. I ain't Hearn's man, but I get along with him. Most of you have lived here for years and you've never had no trouble with him. Why start some now?"

"By God, it's time!" Billy Goat Pete said vehemently. "It's like Hugh says. Any of us can get the same medicine his pa did. What I'm saying right now will probably get me killed, but I'm going to say it. I want to run cattle. All of us would make a better living if we did, and Vic Hearn ain't got the right to say I can or I can't."

"That's right," Prentice agreed. "Most of us have got families. We make a mighty poor living the way it is. A few dollars from cattle would make the difference between scraping the bottom of the barrel all the time like we do, or giving our kids what they need. It would mean more money spent in your store, too, Bob."

"Maybe," Orley said. "But what I'm saying is that we've got along for years, and I don't like the idea of a gunslinging trouble-maker like Moberly riding into the valley and raising hell. Maybe getting us killed if he keeps it up. When you get right down to cases, there ain't a man in this bunch who will stand up against Vic Hearn except

Moberly, and he's dead."

"I may not be the only dead one," Hugh said. "Frank Clemens never got home last night."

They stared at him, shocked into silence by the implication of what he'd said. Billy Goat Pete pointed to a little man on the other side of the circle. "You'd be the last to see Frank, Carl. He was headed east from my place."

The little man fidgeted, then blurted, "I dunno nothing 'bout it."

"When did you see him?" Hugh demanded.

"Little after ten last night. Told me 'bout the meeting here this morning."

"Which way did he go after he left your place?" Hugh asked.

The little man scraped a worn toe through the dust. Finally he said, "East."

"Toward H Ranch?" Hugh asked.

The little man nodded.

"I reckon you'll want to ask Vic about it," Orley said with satisfaction. "Well, you're going to get your chance. Here he comes."

Chapter 27

Hugh whirled with the rest. A man and woman were in a wagon. A second man on a horse rode beside the woman. They were still some distance from town, and it took a moment for Hugh to identify them. Then he saw that his mother and Slim Lee were in the wagon and that Vic Hearn was the horseman.

The men in the street were silent, shocked by Hearn's appearance, coming just at the time when they had been talking about bringing cattle into the valley. Several of them backed toward their horses, then stopped when Billy Goat Pete called, "You ain't leaving. None of you."

Two questions prodded Hugh's mind. Why was Hearn bringing Hugh's mother to town, and why was she riding in a wagon instead of Hearn's buggy, which would have been more comfortable? He didn't have the answers to either, but he was convinced that Hearn hadn't heard what had happened to

Shagnasty Bob and Curly Holt.

Perhaps Hearn had assumed that Hugh was dead, and that his men had done the job they had been sent to town to do. Whatever the man's thinking was, Hugh was sure of one thing: Hearn would not have brought Clara Moberly to town if he expected to find Hugh here.

Dutch Myers wheeled to face Hugh, pulling a derringer as he turned. "You ain't gonna gun Hearn down the way you did —"

Hugh's right hand knocked Myers' arm aside. The derringer went off, the bullet burying itself in the street dust. Hugh hit the man with his left, a sledging blow that sent him sprawling into Bob Orley's arms.

"The next man who tries that will get a bullet," Hugh said. "This is between Hearn and me. Stay out of it! All of you."

Hugh ran toward the hotel, knowing he could count on no help from anyone in the street except possibly Billy Goat Pete. He didn't want help, but he wished there was someone he could trust who would see there was no interference. Dutch Myers might not be the only man who would try to curry favor with Hearn by shooting Hugh Moberly. It would be Oscar Phipps' size, Hugh thought, if the exforeman could get his hands on a gun.

Hugh called, "Ira!" when he reached the hotel. The old man wasn't in sight, but Ellie ran out of the dining room. "My mother's coming with Hearn and Slim Lee," Hugh told Ellie. "Do what you can to take care of her."

Ellie nodded. She was afraid, Hugh knew, but she wasn't backing off. As Ira came along the hall, Hugh turned to him. "Get your Winchester. I don't need any help with Hearn. Just keep the wolfpack off my neck."

Like Ellie, Ira was afraid, but he didn't back off, either. He said, "I'll get it," and turned to the desk. He swore. "It's gone, Hugh. Somebody stole it. I left it in the corner back of the desk."

Hugh, his eyes on the old man, did not doubt what he said. Oscar Phipps had the rifle. It had to be him. In a few minutes Hugh would be in the street facing Vic Hearn, and when that moment came Oscar Phipps would be upstairs in Jean's room overlooking the street.

Neither Hugh Moberly nor anyone else could be fast enough with a gun to cut Vic Hearn down and then get Phipps. There was Slim Lee, too, who had to be kept out of the fight. The townsmen? He wasn't sure. All he knew as he weighed the odds was the fact that the one man in the valley he could count on was Frank Clemens, and Frank Clemens wasn't here.

Hugh gave Ellie a tight grin. He said again, "Do what you can for Ma," and stepped back through the doorway.

Hearn had dismounted and was tying his horse on the other side of the street. Slim Lee was pulling the team to a stop just as Hugh stepped out of the hotel. Clara saw him, and cried out, "Hugh! Hugh!"

He ran to her, thinking that she had aged ten years in the weeks since he had seen her. He put his arms up and helped her down from the wagon seat, and she began to cry. She kissed him, her fingers digging convulsively into his back, then said, "Vic kept telling me you were gone." She tipped her head back. "You're all right, Hugh? You're sure you're all right?"

"I'm fine," he said, and led her to Ellie, who stood in front of the hotel. When he turned toward Hearn, he saw a canvas spread over something in the bed of the wagon.

If Hearn was shocked, or even surprised at seeing Hugh, he gave no indication of it. Hugh didn't expect him to. Hearn had always been one to hide his feelings and his thoughts, and now, his eyes meeting Hugh's, he gave a short nod. He walked to the wagon, asking, "What's the gathering for?"

"Frank Clemens called a meeting," Billy Goat Pete said. "We're fixing to throw in together to buy a herd of cattle. We figure there's plenty of grass in the valley and we won't be interfering with you none."

Pete had taken his rifle from the scabbard. As far as Hugh could see, Pete was the only man in the crowd who was armed. Now Hearn, stopping beside the wagon, said, "That's a bad idea, old man, and you know it damned well. You've got short legs. Don't try to take big steps with 'em."

Hugh walked toward Pete, angling away from Hearn. Of all the men who had obeyed Frank Clemens' call for a meeting, only Billy Goat Pete had any real core of courage. Hugh glanced up at the window of Jean Phipps' room. Her father was standing there. Hugh thought he could see a rifle in his hands. If Pete could at least keep Slim Lee out of the fight, Hugh had a chance.

Hearn threw back the canvas in the wagon bed. "I'm surprised you boys would even talk about fetching in a herd of cattle. You don't need to count on Clemens' big mouth boosting your courage. He tried taking long steps and he's dead. I shot him early this morning."

Though Hugh had been sure Clemens was dead, as sure as he could have been of anything he hadn't actually seen with his own eyes, he was still shocked. The hope that he had been wrong had lingered in him, yet now he knew he had held to it only because he'd wanted to be wrong.

As Hearn's bold gaze raked the crowd, he said, "I don't know what's got into you, or what got into Clemens. He broke into my house early this morning and tried to kill me. I had nothing against him, but I'm damned if I'll stand still in my own house and let a man murder me."

Again there was silence. Hugh wasn't sure what the men standing behind Billy Goat Pete were thinking. He didn't look at them. He kept his eyes on Hearn, waiting for him to make the first move. Hearn must know that this was the finish for one of them, but with supreme self-confidence Hearn did not doubt that it would be Hugh's finish.

Hugh had not glanced at the hotel porch, thinking his mother was inside with Ellie, but now he heard Clara's voice, clear and convincing: "He lies! Clemens came into the kitchen when I first got up this morning. He said he had been waiting for a light because he wanted to see me. He said Hugh was here, that Vic Hearn had killed my husband, and that if I wanted to leave with him, I could. Then Vic shot him. Clemens wasn't armed. It was murder."

Hugh looked at his mother. She stood one step from the door, Ellie beside her. He could not remember seeing his mother stand as straight as she was now, her head held high, her eyes on the crowd of men in the street. As surprised as Hugh was by what she had said, he was even more surprised by the sudden roar that went up from the crowd, a roar that was animal-like in its ferocity. As the men started toward Hearn, Bob Orley's voice rose above the others. "He murdered Frank! I'll get a rope."

And Ted Prentice, "Hang the bastard! I'll put the rope on his neck myself."

"Hold on!" Hugh shouted. "Damn it, move back!"

But no word could have held them back. Nothing short of Frank Clemens' murder could have turned them into a lynch mob. It happened within a matter of seconds, happened so fast that neither Hugh nor anyone else on the street could have stopped it. But Oscar Phipps could, and did. He fired from the window of Jean's room, the bullet kicking up dust between Hearn and the crowd.

"Get back!" Phipps yelled. "Get back, or

the next slug stops the front man." The crowd obeyed, eyes on Phipps, who was leaning out of the window. "That's better. Slim, don't make a move to side Hearn or I'll kill you. Get into the seat. Drive the wagon out of the way. The rest of you back up some more."

The feral fury which had so suddenly possessed the crowd did not go out of it, but Orley and Prentice and the others who were in front had no desire to commit suicide. One glance at Phipps told them that was exactly what they would be doing if they didn't obey him. Slowly the crowd edged back to the side of the street. Lee stepped into the wagon and picked up the lines.

Hearn looked up at Phipps, grinning. "Thanks, Oscar. Loyalty is something I always reward."

"To hell with you!" Phipps shouted in an agonized voice. "You'll never reward me for anything. Moberly wanted a chance at you, and by God he's going to get it! If he don't kill you, I will!"

As the wagon ground past Hugh, Vic Hearn, perhaps for the first time in his life, stood alone. He cuffed his hat back, a strand of yellow hair plastered by sweat against his forehead. There was no fear in him, no doubt. His gaze swung from Clara to Hugh and on to the crowd strung out along the far side of the street, his face showing nothing but scorn.

Once more he looked up at Phipps. "I fire 'em and Moberly hires 'em. That it?"

"No," Hugh said. "This is between you and me. It's been that way for a long time. My only mistake was in waiting."

For a few seconds there was no sound, no movement except for some dust picked up by a sudden gust of wind. In this brief interval of time Hugh's mind went back over the years he had hated Vic Hearn, to his boyhood when Hearn had tried to hold him on his lap and buy his affection with presents, and down to the evening he'd ridden into the place on the Deschutes and learned that his folks were coming here. He had known then he should kill Hearn, but he'd held back because of his mother, and now it was no good to say he'd been wrong, for it changed nothing.

Hugh stood alone just as Hearn stood alone. Their eyes met, Hearn big and self-confident, Hugh knowing that he might die in the next second, but that if he did he would take Hearn with him. For his father, for Frank Clemens, for Ellie. For himself, too, his thoughts turning briefly to the beating he had taken in Hearn's barn.

Suddenly a great anger shattered Hearn's self-control, and he broke the silence with a curse and began to run toward Hugh. Then the foolishness of his act must have occurred to him, for he stopped, shouting, "The waiting was my mistake, not yours!"

Hearn made his play, the fast draw of a man who was as sure of himself at this vital moment as he had been sure of himself through every second of his life. Hearn fired at almost the same instant Hugh did, the explosions coming so close that one seemed a continuation of the other.

Hugh felt the shock of the buck of his gun, the breath of Hearn's bullet on his face. He heard the roar of the two shots, the echoes flung into the street by the buildings that lined it. He pronged back the hammer of his gun, but he didn't fire again.

As Hearn went down to his knees, he fought to hold himself in an upright position. Blood bubbled from his mouth and flowed down his chin. He still held his gun, and now he tried to lift it; but it was too heavy, for strength had run out of him. He toppled forward, his hat falling off his head, and in the sharp morning sunlight his yellow hair seemed very bright.

A sound came from the crowd, a faint sibilant sound of escaping breath. Hugh strode forward and rolled Hearn over on his back; then he eased down the hammer of his gun, and slipped the gun into its holster. He turned to the crowd.

"Take Frank inside," he said, and then motioned toward the dead man at his feet. "Lee, put this in the wagon and haul it back to the ranch."

Orley and Prentice and some of the others rushed to obey his order. Lifting Frank Clemens' body from the wagon, they gently carried it into the hotel. As Hugh watched them, he wanted to tell them that there went a great and good man whose place would never be filled by anyone else. But he could say nothing. His throat ached with the fullness that was in it. There was no reason for talk. They knew, every man there knew what Frank Clemens had been, and they knew, as well as Hugh did, that he had left a vacancy that would never be filled.

As Hugh walked toward the hotel, Phipps met him. Hugh said, "Thanks, Phipps."

"No need to," Phipps said. "Like I told him, I'd have killed him if you hadn't. Not for myself, but for Jean." He wet his lips, then he said, "H Ranch goes to your mother. Hearn put it in his will quite a while ago."

"We don't want it," Hugh said with

sudden violence. "Neither one of us."

"You can't let it go," Phipps said. "Too many people depend on it. It would wreck the valley. There'd be stealing and killing, with everybody grabbing. You've got to hold it together, Moberly."

"Then you're foreman," Hugh said. "You know the ranch and the crew. Take care of it."

Phipps nodded. "If that's the way you want it."

Hugh went past him into the lobby. His mother sat in a rocking chair, her hands folded on her lap. Ellie stood behind her with an arm on Clara's shoulder. Hugh pulled up a chair and sat down beside his mother.

"We're going back to our place on the Deschutes, Ma," he said. "Ellie and her dad and you and me. I'll ride out to H Ranch and get the wagon. Is there anything you want?"

She acted as if she hadn't understood. She simply sat there, staring and apparently seeing nothing. Then she said, "I killed your father, Hugh. Mama used to tell me I lived in my dreams too much. Sam said the same, and now I know what they meant. I made a dream about Vic. It was such a good dream that I never really saw him until he shot Frank Clemens."

"We've got a lot of good years ahead of us, Mrs. Moberly," Ellie said. "We've got to think of them and not of the ones that are behind us."

"Sometimes dreaming is a good thing, Ma," Hugh said. "Like Pa's dream about his timber. It'll come true. You'll see."

Clara smiled a little then, and reached up and patted Ellie's hand. "Yes," she said. "Sam's dream was a good dream. I'm sorry that I didn't know."

Hugh looked up at Ellie, who smiled assurance at him. The good years ahead and the good dreams. Wherever he was, Sam Moberly would know.

About the Author

Wayne D. Overholser has won three Golden Spur awards from the Western Writers of America and has a long list of fine Western titles to his credit. He was born in Pomeroy, Washington, and attended the University of Montana, University of Oregon, and the University of Southern California before becoming a public school teacher and principal in various Oregon communities. He began writing for Western pulp magazines in 1936 and within a couple of years was a regular contributor to Street & Smith's *Western Story* and Fiction House's *Lariat Story Magazine. Buckaroo's Code* (1948) was his first Western novel and remains one of his best. In the 1950s and 1960s, having retired from academic work to concentrate on writing, he would publish as many as four books a year under his own name or a pseudonym, most prominently as Joseph Wayne. *The Bitter Night, The Lone Deputy,* and *The Violent Land* are among the finest of the early Overholser titles. He was asked by William MacLeod Raine, that dean among Western writers, to complete his last novel after Raine's death. Some of Overholser's most rewarding novels were actually collaborations with other Western writers: *Colorado Gold* with Chad Merriman and *Showdown at Stony Creek* with Lewis B. Patten. Overholser's Western novels, no matter under what name they have been published, are based on a solid knowledge of the history and customs of the American frontier West, particularly when set in his two favorite Western states, Oregon and Colorado. When it comes to his characters, he writes with skill, an uncommon sensitivity, and a consistently vivid and accurate vision of a way of life unique in human history.

We hope you have enjoyed this Large Print book. Other Thorndike, Wheeler or Chivers Press Large Print books are available at your library or directly from the publishers.

For more information about current and upcoming titles, please call or write, without obligation, to:

Publisher
Thorndike Press
295 Kennedy Memorial Drive
Waterville, ME   04901
Tel. (800) 223-1244

Or visit our Web site at:
www.gale.com/thorndike
www.gale.com/wheeler

OR

Chivers Large Print
published by BBC Audiobooks Ltd
St James House, The Square
Lower Bristol Road
Bath BA2 3SB
England
Tel. +44(0) 800 136919
email: bbcaudiobooks@bbc.co.uk
www.bbcaudiobooks.co.uk

All our Large Print titles are designed for easy reading, and all our books are made to last.